Mail Order Faith

Book Three of
Mail Order Bluebonnet Brides

Charlotte Dearing

Author's note: You should know what you're getting… I write clean, wholesome love stories set in late 19th century Texas. The hero is strong, successful, and flawed, in ways he doesn't realize until he meets the heroine. In the end, my heroes and heroines find a path to happiness through perseverance and faith.

Chapter One

Faith O'Brian

Faith arranged the pastries and tea cakes on the finest, most delicate blue willow China plates. She knew the guests waited for her in the parlor, wanting their refreshments, so she worked quickly. Too quickly, it turned out. One of the petit fours tumbled off the plate to the floor and rolled under the kitchen table.

"Drat," she muttered.

"Allow me, Miss O'Brian."

Startled, Faith couldn't stop a panicked yelp. It was Phipps, the butler. She hadn't realized he had entered the kitchen. Mrs. Caldicott probably sent him to find out why she was taking so long.

Phipps crawled under the table, promptly banging his head. The impact of his balding head smacking against the table jostled the neatly stacked cakes and cookies. Another petit four fell off the plate, directly in the path of the butler.

"Watch out for the-" Faith said. Her warning came too late. Phipps mashed the cake under his knee. "Oh, dear."

He grumbled a few words under his breath and Faith worried that he might be cross with her. She always tried to keep her eyes averted around Phipps or any of the other male staff, never certain when she might get an attack of nerves. She held her breath, praying he wouldn't be angry for the trouble she'd caused, but when he emerged from under the table, he wore a triumphant smile and brandished the petit four like a hard-won prize.

"Found it!"

He rubbed his head, and looked so pleased with himself, Faith couldn't bear to tell him that another cake was plastered to the knee of his trousers.

Mrs. Caldicott's voice came from the parlor. "What on earth is taking her so long?"

Phipps shrugged good-naturedly as he dropped the errant petit four in the rubbish bin. Faith moved to the plates, intending to carry them into the parlor, but he waved her off. She retreated several steps to give him a wide berth. Not that Phipps was a dangerous man, or even rough-tempered. She simply always avoided him as much as possible. He was a good twenty years older than her, and always cordial. Despite that, she still fretted anytime he smiled or bid her good morning. At times, her nervousness around men would make her start hiccupping, or blushing red like a tomato, or otherwise turning into a ninny.

"Allow me, Miss O'Brian." He gave a slight bow, wincing as he straightened.

"Thank you."

She followed him down the corridor to the sitting room, took a seat near the fireplace and accepted a cup of tea from the servant. Her hand trembled. The teacup rattled. Hastily, she set it down beside her and stole a glance at Phipps. The cake smeared against his pants no longer resembled cake. It was just a white streak of icing with a few crumbs clinging to the fabric.

She hiccupped. Mrs. Caldicott turned her way, her brow knit. Faith coughed in an attempt to disguise her fretfulness. She wasn't shy by nature, but in the last few months she'd grown reticent and nervous, especially around men. Perhaps it was all part of the absurd plan she'd agreed to. Her sister in Texas, Grace, had proposed the idea that she write to Grace's brother-in-law and consider joining him in marriage. Faith had been so desperate to see Grace that she'd agreed to the foolhardy scheme.

Now she wished she'd just stayed put in Boston, working as Mrs. Caldicott's companion. It was far less risky. Well, to be clear, it wasn't risky at all. She hiccupped again.

"Are you all right, dear?" Mrs. Caldicott asked under her breath.

Faith gave a slight nod. Mrs. Caldicott sighed and turned back to her friends. She perched precariously on the edge of the over-stuffed sofa, surrounded by two ladies from church, tut-tutting about the perils of Texas.

Mrs. Caldicott spoke. "I told Faith she can't possibly run off to marry a man she's never met."

Her friends, elderly ladies who visited every Sunday afternoon, nodded in agreement and sipped their tea. They looked alarmed, their complexions growing even more pale.

Faith managed a small smile. "Thomas and I have written several letters. I haven't agreed to marry him, just to travel to Texas to see my sister and make his acquaintance."

"Good heavens," Mrs. Caldicott said tragically. "You'll find a countryside teeming with thieves and cutthroats."

"Rattlesnakes and robbers," Mrs. Hurst proclaimed.

"And ruffians," Mrs. Whipple added, giving Faith a look of distress over her China teacup. "Don't forget the ruffians."

Mrs. Whipple's attendant giggled. "It sounds like a grand adventure."

There was a collective gasp of surprise from the ladies.

"I don't intend to go for the adventure," Faith assured the ladies. "I don't believe in adventure."

The ladies nodded in unison.

"I'm the unadventurous sister," Faith said quietly. "But I am the sister with excellent judgment, and I need to see Grace with my own eyes to assure myself that she's safe. I may be unadventurous, but I am a good judge of character."

Unadventurous was putting it mildly. Everyone knew that Faith was the boring sister. The sensible sister. Secretly, she'd indulged in reading books about steadfast cowboys and daring heroines, but she'd never admit to the wild imaginings the stories stirred inside her heart.

She didn't yearn for adventure. Not at all. She felt she *must* travel to Texas. Once there, Faith would be able to determine if her sister was, in fact, doing well. Faith and Hope, her younger sister and roommate, suspected that Grace wrote letters under duress. She claimed to be happy, but her wicked husband probably forced her to write letters praising her new home.

Grace, considered by all to be the kind sister, had been in Texas several months now and wrote letters boasting of its beauty, the wide-open spaces and the clean fresh air.

Faith wasn't certain what to believe of her sister's letters. Grace had traveled to Texas as a mail-order bride in the spring. She'd arrived to find that her husband, John, the man she'd married by proxy, had died from the bite of a venomous snake. After that, Grace had sent several letters, each more bewildering than the one before.

At first Grace wrote to say that she intended to stay to care for John's infant daughter. Then she wrote that her brother-in-law insisted she marry him. In the last letter, Grace explained she was blissfully happy, married, and caring for the orphaned baby.

Faith intended to see for herself.

She vowed to get on a train as soon as Mrs. Caldicott hired a new companion. Once Mrs. Caldicott was situated, Faith would journey to Texas. She'd explained her plan to Hope. Faith told her that she wanted... no, needed to see that Grace was well. Hope hadn't agreed to any part of the plan.

Of course, she hadn't.

Everyone knew Hope was the stubborn sister.

"I offered to double her pay," Mrs. Caldicott said wistfully. "I'm so attached to my sweet Faith."

The other ladies nodded in agreement.

"Perhaps the sister can take her place," Mrs. Whipple offered.

Faith shook her head. "Hope works at a bookstore. I can't imagine her ever wanting another position."

"Poor girl," Mrs. Caldicott murmured. "She might be left behind, all by herself."

"If I had my choice, I'd take her with me," Faith said. "I'd prefer not to make the trip alone. Once I arrive in Texas, I plan to send for her."

"Doesn't your sister have another brother-in-law?" asked Mrs. Whipple. She nibbled a tea cake.

"Yes. She does. He's written to my younger sister, but she refused to write him back."

"Sensible girl," Mrs. Whipple said.

"You might be right," Faith said. "The men of that family seem to be quite overbearing. He wrote her a second time, dropping casual comments about coming to Boston to whisk her away."

The ladies stared with wordless disbelief. For a long moment, no one spoke. Faith blushed at the expressions of shock and sympathy. Mrs. Caldicott, noting her embarrassment, filled Faith's teacup, waving off the servant.

"There, there, my dear, as much as I hate to lose you, I'm sure it will all work out for the best, for all three of you girls. I'm certain that you are braver than you know."

Faith blushed at the praise.

Mrs. Caldicott went on. "I hope you don't mind if I change the subject. Did Phipps talk to you?"

Faith blinked in surprise and turned to the butler who stood at the door. His posture was ramrod straight and he held his hands behind his back. He too looked surprised. His brows lifted and ears tinged with pink.

"I hadn't yet, Mrs. Caldicott. I didn't want to impose on Miss O'Brian while we had company."

"Come, Phipps. I'd like the ladies to see the gift you have for your granddaughter."

Faith drew a sharp breath, hardly able to imagine where the conversation might turn next.

Phipps, looking sheepish, pulled a small bundle from his breast pocket. As he crossed the room, he slowly and with infinite care, unwrapped the tissue. He held it out for the ladies to inspect. Nestled in the tissue was a lace handkerchief. The fabric had dulled from age. Faith was certain it had once been white, but now was closer to ivory.

"This belonged to my dear Lillian. Her father gave it to her when she turned ten. My granddaughter will turn ten next month, and I intend to give it to her."

A murmur of approval moved through the group.

He moved toward Faith, so she could better see the antique lace.

"It's beautiful, Phipps," she murmured. "It's a filet lace."

"The edge is tattered," he said quietly but with a hint of wanting to say more.

"Would you like me to mend it for you?" Faith asked.

The man's eyes shone wistfully. "I think Lillian would have been so pleased, and I would be so very grateful."

His voice shook with emotion and Faith's heart went out to the man. She knew he was a widower. She'd heard him speak of his wife, always in glowing terms. The uneasiness she'd felt earlier disappeared like morning dew on a summer morning. The love he felt for his late wife practically shone from his expression. What would it be like to be so loved by one's husband? Her breath caught. She couldn't find the words to reply.

As usual, Mrs. Caldicott seemed to sense her every emotion. She covered Faith's hands with hers.

"Faith, my dear, bring your tools and materials tomorrow," Mrs. Caldicott said with a warm smile. "You can do your work here in the parlor. I'd like to watch you spin your lace. It might be my last chance."

Chapter Two

Thomas Bentley

The setting sun cast long shadows around Thomas and Caleb as they stood before the grave. The last rays of sunshine lit the damp headstone with a soft glow that brought a smile to Caleb's lips. Thomas couldn't help smiling at his son and tousling his hair. The boy had spent the better part of an hour scrubbing the headstone. Satisfaction lit his eyes.

"What was my mother like?" Caleb asked.

She was a liar...

"Very pretty," Thomas said. "She loved animals just like you. That's where you get your gift from – your momma."

Caleb's grin faded, he sniffed, pulled a handkerchief from his pocket and wiped his eyes. "Don't tell anyone that I get misty sometimes, okay? 'Specially not Uncle Lucas."

"Of course not, son. It's no one's concern. A boy is entitled to get a little teary-eyed on his mother's birthday. Especially if she passed away when he was just a baby."

"I think about her all the time."

"Why, sure you do."

"You miss her too?"

Caleb turned to him and Thomas knew the boy searched his expression for a sign of grief. Much as he tried to appear sorrowful, Thomas was certain he didn't quite manage the look very well. Caleb had just turned eleven a few days before.

He was growing like a weed and Thomas worried there would come a day when the boy saw through his false words.

Thomas had always prided himself on his honesty, but he'd told a wagonload of lies ever since Lorena died. He told himself the lies were necessary. A kindness. He prayed that Caleb would never find out the truth.

"Mostly, I try not to think about your mother."

Caleb nodded. "It hurts too much."

Thomas winced. "That's right." He set his hand on his son's shoulder and pulled him next to him.

The boy wrapped his arm around his waist, giving him a rare hug. Caleb liked to pride himself on being grown. Whenever they were with the ranch cowboys, Caleb tried to act tough, but when it was just the two of them, the boy allowed Thomas to treat him with some tenderness.

"Do you suppose Faith will let me call her momma?" Caleb asked.

"I don't know, son. I can write her and ask."

Caleb shook his head. "I was thinking, I could write her and ask myself."

"All right."

Thomas forced himself to use a cheerful tone even though he felt like gritting his teeth. When he first wrote to Faith, he thought she'd welcome his letters and his invitation to Texas. Instead, she seemed to think he and his brothers were of questionable moral fiber. She'd written those very words because of the way Matt had practically forced Grace to marry him.

Thomas had to admit, Matt's marriage to Grace had been slightly coerced, but he'd married her to keep her safe from the rougher elements in Magnolia. The marriage was meant to be an arrangement. Nothing more.

They'd argued plenty in the beginning, but now they were happy as could be. Something must have changed. Their marriage was definitely not *just* an arrangement. Just yesterday they announced they had a little one on the way. Thomas wouldn't allow himself to hope for that sort of happiness. All he wanted was a wife to help raise Caleb. Nothing more. He wouldn't ever allow a woman to betray his trust again. He'd learned his lesson the first time around.

The hard way.

"What do you say we go home and have some supper?" Thomas asked.

"Is Uncle Lucas cooking?"

"Try not to sound so pleased."

"I get tired of scrambled eggs."

Thomas got tired of his brother's scrambled eggs too, but not tired enough to volunteer to cook. He and his brother lived in the same ranch house along with Caleb. The house was built right in the middle of the Bentley pastures. Neither Lucas nor Thomas especially liked living under the same roof. They were too set in their ways, but that's the way things were, for now.

"Besides, Uncle Lucas burns the eggs every time," Caleb insisted.

"Make yourself a fried egg sandwich."

"I get tired of those too."

"Either is better than going hungry."

Caleb sighed and looked downcast. "Yes, sir."

They returned to their horses and mounted. Thomas grimaced at the pain in his shoulder. A cattle rustler had gotten a lucky shot and hit him in the shoulder a few months prior. The ball had gone straight through. Doc had fixed him up, but every so often his shoulder pained him.

More than ever, the injury had convinced him that taking a wife was the right thing to do. He needed a wife in case he ever got hurt. He didn't want to leave Caleb in his brothers' care even though both men loved Caleb like a son.

They rode away from Lorena's grave, Thomas giving it a final glance. He always felt a sense of relief when they left this place. While Caleb came to his mother's grave frequently, Thomas only made the trip up the ridge once a year. The rest of the time, he avoided the area. Today, he'd done his duty, managed to keep up the appearance of the grieving widow for one more year. By this time next year, he'd be married again, God-willing. He wondered if Faith would want to accompany him and Caleb for the annual visit.

Probably not. And who could blame her?

They rode down the ridge single file, with Caleb leading the way. The boy rode his gelding, sitting tall in the saddle, his narrow, boyish build making Thomas's heart squeeze with pain. His son yearned for a mother's love more than anything in the world. Caleb wanted a family and had even asked about brothers and sisters.

Thomas was sure there'd be no children. He hadn't said so explicitly, but he'd suggested that his and Faith's marriage would be a mutually beneficial arrangement. He'd gone so far as to tell her she would have her own room. Despite the plan, he prayed Faith would show Caleb some of the love he so badly needed. In his mind, Thomas imagined Faith to be a warm-hearted woman like Grace. And yet, he'd been fooled before. While he knew he could withstand anything that came his way, he couldn't bear the notion of Caleb getting hurt.

His thoughts warred against each other.

On one hand, he was sure Faith would love Caleb right off. Sure, the boy was a little uncouth. He didn't care much for regular baths and sometimes wiped his mouth with his sleeve. Often. Maybe always, come to think of it.

On the other hand, he was a hard worker, gentle with animals and generally sensitive to those around him. He seemed to have a sense about people and animals that set him apart from others. He knew how to calm a skittish yearling. He was an expert at teaching a mutt tricks of all kinds, and no one could make Harriet Patchwell, Matt and Grace's cook, and a notorious curmudgeon, laugh as readily as Caleb.

Mrs. Patchwell doted on the boy.

Matt and Grace's home sat in a meadow below them. A ribbon of smoke spiraled from the chimney. The homey sight gave Thomas a twinge of jealousy as he imagined his brother and sister-in-law gathering around the dinner table. As they drew closer, the aroma of Mrs. Patchwell's pot roast drifted through the air.

Caleb turned in his saddle, giving him a pleading look.

"We've eaten there twice this week, son."

"I'm a growing boy."

"Don't I know it."

Thomas eyed his son's shirt collar, noting the wrinkles. His sleeves were too short. His shirt was untucked. The boy looked like a young street urchin and Mrs. Patchwell would waste no time announcing that to the world.

"Besides, Mrs. Patchwell is probably missing me," Caleb said. "You know how much she loves seeing me."

The aroma grew stronger as they descended. Thomas's stomach rumbled. His mouth watered as he imagined the savory meat and potatoes, and the rich gravy. As much as he hated showing up with Caleb at dinnertime like a pair of starving wolves, he couldn't imagine going home to eat whatever Lucas had thrown together.

If they kept riding, they could take the back way and get home by nightfall. If they stopped now, they'd have to take the road which would take longer. There was going to be a full moon, but the moonlight wouldn't be enough to safely trek along the rough paths along the back of the ranch. Still, the longer route was worth it. Harriet Patchwell's cooking was the best he'd ever known.

He scrubbed a hand across his unshaven jaw. Likely he didn't look much better than Caleb, although Harriet Patchwell wouldn't ever say a word about his appearance. He squinted, studying the front of the ranch house.

"Why, that rascal," Thomas muttered.

"What is it?"

"Your Uncle Lucas's horse is tied to the hitching rail."

Caleb gave a whoop and spurred his horse into a trot. When they reached the bottom of the ridge, he loped the rest of the way to the house. Thomas followed close behind. They hitched their horses and went inside the house. The fragrance of freshly baked bread almost brought a tear to Thomas's eye. Caleb hurried down the hallway and into the kitchen.

When Thomas heard Mrs. Patchwell's gasp, he couldn't hold back a grin.

"Merciful heavens," she shrieked. "This poor boy needs a mother in the worst way."

Chapter Three

Faith

Faith and Hope traipsed through the rose gardens, following Mrs. Caldicott as she pruned the rose bushes. The flowers, always glorious throughout the summer, offered their last blooms as autumn winds turned cooler. Since Mrs. Caldicott and her husband never had children, they'd devoted their time to the tremendous gardens that surrounded the Caldicott house.

As they walked, they chatted about the stew Faith had made for dinner the night before.

"My sister is a dreadful cook," Hope teased, her lips curving into a taunting smile as she kept her gaze on Faith. "She can hardly boil water."

Faith shook her head. "You're a fine one to talk. You had three helpings of the stew I made last night."

Mrs. Caldicott laughed as she snipped a spent bloom. "I'm certain you're wrong. I've tasted Faith's cooking and found it excellent."

Faith arched her brow to give her sister a chastising look, barely able to hold back a smile. Hope was cheeky, to be sure. The two of them had a small rivalry and enjoyed competing to see who sewed the finest stitches, baked the flakiest pie crust, or who had the straightest posture. Before Grace had left Boston, there were two sisters Faith had to contend with. In

Grace's absence, Hope had taken up the slack, teasing Faith every chance she got.

Hope spent her days amidst books, reading them, selling them, talking about them. She probably dreamed of the stories she read. She'd embraced her work in the bookshop with complete devotion. Both sisters had left the lace-making shops, improving their lot with new work in a better part of town. They no longer had to walk past beggars or pickpockets. They shared a room between the book shop and Mrs. Caldicott's home.

Mrs. Caldicott walked along the hedges, snipping blooms and handing them over her shoulder to Faith. When they had enough for a small bouquet for the parlor, they turned indoors. Just in time too. The skies turned a dark, ominous grey.

A quarter hour later, they sat in Mrs. Caldicott's parlor sipping tea. Outside it rained, a steady downpour that drummed on the windows. Hope had joined them that morning to bring Mrs. Caldicott several new books, but when it began to drizzle, Mrs. Caldicott used the weather as an excuse for Hope to sit a spell and have some tea.

The sound of the gentle rain, along with the soft crackle of the blaze in the fireplace, made for a cozy afternoon. Faith felt a rush of warmth and happiness, but just as suddenly that contentment fell away as a new feeling took its place. With a start, she realized that she would leave this all behind when she went to Texas. Of course, she knew this all along, but in that moment the notion of leaving presented itself in whole new, stark reality.

Her old fears lurked in the shadows of her mind. What if Thomas was as quick to anger as her father? What if Grace's husband was too, despite her cheery letters? The possibility frightened her. She could easily evade Thomas's marriage offer, but what of her sister?

Her eyes prickled with tears as she watched Hope chat with Mrs. Caldicott. Her sister's animated face always took on a lovely shade of pink whenever she began talking about the bookshop. She told Mrs. Caldicott about the books she'd read in the last week. A considerable number, even for Hope.

A wave of loneliness swept over Faith. She'd soon see Grace, and was glad of that, but she'd say goodbye to so much. And there was the possibility that Hope would refuse to join her and Grace in Texas. After one letter from Lucas, Hope seemed less sure of the plan to travel to Texas.

Faith wondered if Hope held some of the same fears she did, the one thing they almost never mentioned – their father's terrible temper. Their father had been in an accident, and their mother claimed that it was his injury that left him prone to fits of rage. Faith wasn't always entirely sure if it was the accident or simply his nature. Her darkest fear was that Grace's husband might have the same fearsome temper.

Grace had never alluded to anything sinister, but her husband had practically forced her to marry him. What sort of man did such a thing? She shivered as frightening possibilities prowled in the shadows of her mind. Part of her fretted that Mrs. Caldicott hadn't found another companion just yet, and another part of her wished she had hired a new girl already. If that were the case, Faith could get on the train tomorrow.

"More tea?" the serving girl asked the ladies.

"Yes, please," Mrs. Caldicott said. "I do enjoy company and hope the rain lasts all afternoon. Could you tell Phipps to mend the fire, Annabelle?"

"Yes, Mrs. Caldicott."

A moment later Phipps came into the parlor. He brightened when he saw Faith and Hope sitting with Mrs. Caldicott.

"How did your granddaughter like her handkerchief?" Mrs. Caldicott asked.

"Very much, Mrs. Caldicott. She said it was the finest gift she'd ever received."

"Of course she did," Mrs. Caldicott said with a distinct air of satisfaction, as if she herself had stitched the tattered edges of the handkerchief. Phipps tossed wood on the fire, stirred the glowing coals with a poker. After a moment he left the parlor, giving Faith a kind smile as he passed.

Hope took a biscuit from the tea service tray. She took a dainty bite. Faith selected one, a jam-filled confection and nibbled the edge.

"Mrs. Caldicott, I'm sure you'll miss my sister almost as much as I will," Hope said. "I'll be sure to come visit and bring you books to fill your days."

"That sounds delightful," Mrs. Caldicott said. "But I'm not sure how soon your sister will depart Boston. She agreed to stay until I find a replacement, and I haven't even started looking."

Faith laughed softly, wondering if that were true. Mrs. Caldicott did love to joke, but she hadn't smiled as she said the words or spoken in a teasing tone. Faith felt her heart thud in her chest and those mixed feelings tightened around her heart. Go... stay... go?

Hope's eyes widened. "Faith didn't work for you last winter, so you couldn't possibly know that she became very ill. In fact, she had to take to her bed for weeks. Grace and I were beside ourselves with worry."

Mrs. Caldicott's lips parted with surprise and she drew a sharp breath. "I didn't know any of this."

Hope nodded, her complexion draining of color.

"It's true," Faith said quietly. "That's the reason Grace went to Texas. To make a way for us... well, to make a way for me."

Hope dropped her gaze, the skin around her mouth growing taut.

"I had no idea," Mrs. Caldicott murmured, an edge of sorrow in her voice. "No idea at all."

Chapter Four

Thomas

A young man hurried up the steps of the sheriff's office, a note in his hand. Thomas had just locked the door and intended to head back to the ranch. He and his brother Matt planned to brand a group of calves that afternoon. The look on the boy's face told him all he needed to know. He'd have to delay his ranch work.

The boy handed him the envelope. Thomas recognized the handwriting as that of Baron Calhoun, the owner of the Magnolia Bank and Trust. Before he could thank the boy, or ask him about the nature of the note, the boy raced off. Thomas shook his head and smiled. Baron was known to be a tough taskmaster and probably had put the fear of God into his errand boy.

The note had a hastily written message, asking Thomas to come to the bank about an urgent matter. Thomas put his cowboy hat on and strolled the two blocks to the bank. The noon sun warmed his shoulders, a welcome change from the prior day's cold snap. Cowboys lined the walk. Yesterday there'd been a sale at the Magnolia auction house, and there were still a few cowboys in town.

By late afternoon, they'd head home to return to work. The town would resume its usual quiet day-to-day business. The auctions, held once a month, always brought visitors.

Sometimes they brought trouble too. Thomas hoped that Baron's note didn't pertain to any problem of that sort. It didn't seem likely. Usually the problems arose when the men had a few too many drinks at the saloon and brawled. Luckily, there hadn't been a single brawl the night before.

He entered the bank, swiping his hat from his head. He passed the windows where the bank tellers helped customers and took the stairs to the offices on the second floor. Mr. Calhoun's assistant met him at the door with a friendly smile. A good sign, Thomas thought. Maybe this wasn't going to be terrible news after all.

Baron sat at his desk, his brow furrowed as he studied a letter. When he saw Thomas, he got to his feet. His brow remained pinched with worry.

"Afternoon." Thomas crossed the room, stopped before the immense mahogany desk and offered his hand.

"Is it afternoon, already?" Baron frowned as he reached across the desk to shake Thomas's hand.

"It is. 'Bout time for supper, I'd say."

Baron snapped open his pocket watch. "I'll be."

"Mr. Bentley," a woman's voice came from behind him.

Thomas turned to find Baron's wife, Emily, standing in the doorway. She wore a gown the color of a summer sky and held a basket. She smiled at him and held the basket up to draw his attention.

"I happened to have brought sandwiches for my husband. He never takes time to eat when he's at the bank unless I set food right in front of him." She sighed. "And then he wonders why he's as hungry as a bear when he comes home in the evenings. I brought plenty. I'd be pleased if you'd have one."

Thomas chuckled, delighted by her offer, and his stomach rumbled its agreement. It seemed he was always hungry. A wave of envy washed over him. Baron was lucky to have such a sweet-natured, lovely wife. Their marriage had been the scandal of Magnolia some months before, when the wealthy, older and surly rancher had taken the shy shop girl as his wife.

"That's very kind of you, Mrs. Calhoun," Thomas said.

He watched Baron Calhoun go to his wife and kiss her cheek. The hard line of the man's mouth curved into a grin as he regarded his pretty wife. Thomas was struck by the change in Baron's demeanor and marveled how Baron seemed as taken with Emily as she was with him.

He forced himself to look away, feeling a twist of resentment inside his chest. Even Baron Calhoun, the grouch of Magnolia, had found a woman to love and who returned his affection. Thomas couldn't imagine a more unlikely situation. Some men were just lucky, he supposed.

"I'll leave you two gentlemen to visit," Emily said. "I have to go to the mercantile to pick up some wool for my knitting project."

"Is that so?" Thomas asked. Normally he wouldn't have commented, but he could tell by the spark in Mrs. Calhoun's eye this was no ordinary task.

She looked up at Baron and blushed.

"You might as well tell folks," Baron said gently as he took the basket from her.

Mrs. Calhoun's blush deepened. "Come spring, Baron and I will welcome our first child."

Thomas managed a smile. "Congratulations to both of you."

Baron nodded. "Thank you." He bent down to kiss his wife again and ushered her to the door.

"Good day, sheriff," she said. Then she turned to her husband, set her hand on his chest and murmured a few parting words. After that, she was gone. The sound of her rustling skirts faded as she departed.

Another twinge of envy burned inside Thomas. For the hundredth time, he tried to imagine what kind of girl Faith was. He could picture her, somewhat, assuming she favored her sister, Grace, and he thought his sister-in-law to be very pretty. But what he wondered about even more was her character. Would she dote on him like Mrs. Calhoun doted on Baron? All along he'd told himself he didn't care, but in a single flash of clarity, he realized he did care. Very much.

He'd just witnessed a small act of tenderness between a husband and wife. The gesture planted a seed inside his heart. The plan to marry Faith had been to offer a better home for Caleb. Thomas knew he'd hate the notion of wanting anything for himself, but there it was, an undeniable yearning.

Turning away, he scrubbed his hand down his face and suppressed a groan of frustration.

Baron unpacked the basket, offered him a sandwich and sat down across from him. "I suppose you're wondering what this is about."

"I imagine it's not just to chat over lunch," Thomas said, accepting a sandwich from Baron.

He sank into a nearby chair, took a bite of the sandwich and sighed contentedly. Suddenly he was not just hungry, but ravenous. He should be listening to Baron, but all he could think about was the way the savory, heavily smoked ham tasted. The bread was delicious too. Fragrant and slightly sweet, it contrasted with the salty ham.

Without waiting for a response, Baron went on. "I recently bought a bank in Fort Worth. It's been in business for about a month now."

"I didn't know you had banking interests outside of Magnolia."

"I do. Probably a poor idea, since I don't care to travel without my wife. Now that she's in the family way, I need to depend on my bank manager to take care of matters."

Thomas only half-listened to Baron talk about his business concerns. He wondered what it had to do with him. He should be heading to the family ranch to pitch in with the branding, not chit-chatting with Baron Calhoun about some bank that was hundreds of miles away.

"I don't usually like mustard on my sandwich, but this is very good," he said. "I wonder if Caleb would like a ham sandwich with mustard. Course, the bread makes the difference, doesn't it? I suppose Emily makes it herself or do you have a cook?"

Baron stared at his sandwich, studying it as if he'd hardly noticed the details before. "I don't rightly know. I never pay attention."

"If you ate any of my brother's cooking, you'd notice that sort of thing."

Baron scratched his head. "Anyhow, the bank manager claims the safe was robbed last Friday."

"Sorry to hear."

"You're probably wondering what that has to do with you."

"Nothing, I'd say, although I'll come talk to you anytime you feed me lunch."

"This is the second robbery in Fort Worth. The thieves made off with quite a bundle, and while I resent the theft, what I want more than the money is the coins they stole."

Thomas waited, wondering where this might go. He finished his sandwich and accepted a glass of lemonade from Baron.

"The thieves have a cabin a few miles out of Magnolia," Baron said.

Thomas grimaced and rubbed the back of his neck. Maybe it was time to retire from being a lawman. He had a pretty good idea who Baron referred to and it wasn't good.

"The Grimes brothers," Thomas muttered. "They're back in town?"

"That's right. We think their older sister is involved. She's in her forties, I'd say, but she's still involved in their schemes. The Pinkerton agent I hired thinks the robbery was committed by one of the clerks who has ties to the Grimes family. The theft was small, likely carried out in broad daylight. A small stash of coins."

Thomas frowned. "Coins?"

"They're very valuable coins. The agent told me the Grimes brothers plan to hightail it to Mexico. The sister wants to give them a little going-away present to make sure they live high on the hog instead of robbing more banks."

Thomas shook his head. "So she stole the coins for her brothers?"

"That's my theory. The coins are small, easy to carry, but worth a mint, especially in Mexico. She's going to bring them to Magnolia soon."

"All right. I don't relish the thought of arresting a lady, but I will if need be."

Baron sat back in his chair, a satisfied smile on his face. "I think she's coming. She's going to get those coins to her brothers somehow before they head south to the port of Galveston."

Thomas didn't ask how Baron knew all this about a pair of men the Texas Rangers had been hunting for years. The man probably had spies all over Texas, protecting his vast wealth.

If he said the Grimes brothers were around Magnolia, Thomas didn't doubt him.

"I'll see what I can do," he said. "Not too many ladies coming to Magnolia. I'll put a deputy at the train station for the next couple of weeks. We'll see if she steps off the four o'clock."

"Promise me you'll arrest her," Baron asked, his mouth tilting into a smile. "You won't feel sorry for her just because she's a woman."

"A criminal is a criminal. If a woman steps off that train with your stolen loot, I'll make certain she faces justice."

Baron gave him a skeptical look. "Really?"

"Of course, I will."

Chapter Five

Faith

The instant Mrs. Caldicott learned of Faith's illness she'd set about to find her replacement. Faith wasn't sure if she was pleased or not. Even though she knew Mrs. Caldicott to be a woman of immense energy and steely determination, part of her felt certain it would take time to find a suitable companion.

To her astonishment and dismay, it took only a couple of days.

She hired a new girl and promptly dismissed Faith. It wasn't done in a heartless way. On the contrary, Mrs. Caldicott grew tearful as she told Faith about the new girl. Faith assured her she could stay longer, but her employer would hear nothing of it.

On what was to be her final evening with Mrs. Caldicott, the woman walked her to the door. She wrapped her in a warm embrace, holding her for a long moment, and whispered a trembling goodbye. When she stepped back, she took Faith's hands in hers and pressed an envelope into her palm.

Faith, still in a state of shock at her dismissal, stared at the envelope, bewildered.

"You, my dear, are embarking on a tremendous journey. I'm giving you a small gift. Some money."

Faith tried to protest, but Mrs. Caldicott waved off her concerns.

"I insist, Faith. I want you to take this money and I want you to promise that you'll buy something for yourself. I know how you always want to do for others, but on this matter, I must have my way. I want you to buy something special that will make your life in Texas more..."

Her words faded. A look of distress came over her.

"More what?" Faith asked.

Mrs. Caldicott shuddered. "More bearable."

"All right," Faith said softly.

"And write to me. Do you promise to write to me? If you arrive and find that your Thomas is monstrous, send me a letter and I'll send you train fare – or I'll come for you myself."

Faith laughed and shook her head. She still felt an overwhelming disbelief and could hardly imagine herself going to Texas, much less the prim Mrs. Caldicott.

"I don't know what to say," Faith whispered.

Mrs. Caldicott lifted her hands to cup Faith's face. She leaned forward and to Faith's surprise the woman's eyes shone with tears.

"I always wanted to go on adventure," she said quietly. "And now I'm too old. You go, my dear Faith. Go and have an adventure for me."

Faith nodded, too overcome to reply. She departed the Caldicott home before she burst into tears. She hurried to the small room she and Hope shared, grateful to find that Hope wasn't home.

In the quiet of their room, she sat on the bed, marveling at the turn of events. Thomas didn't expect her for another month, at least. She took out a sheet of writing paper, intending to tell him about her change of plans. She sat at her desk, with her pen and ink, trying to find a way to tell him that she was on her way.

The clock on the bedside table ticked steadily as she stared at the blank page. If she wrote to him, he might see it as a sign of her commitment to him. He'd pressed her for a promise to come to Texas. He also requested permission to call on her, right away, with the hope of marrying as soon as possible. His son needed a mother. She should feel some warmth for the motherless child but couldn't imagine a boy would welcome a stranger in his home.

Her father's words rang in her ears. *Of all the terrible luck – three children and not one of them a son to carry on my name...*

The shouting was always followed by the crash of dishes or a chair. He'd throw anything he could get his hands on. He never intended to strike his family, but that didn't mean it didn't happen. She tugged her sleeve up her arm. Even in the dim, afternoon light the scar was clearly visible, an ugly reminder of her father's terrifying outbursts.

Her valise sat in the corner, mocking all her brave intentions. Thomas had wanted to send money, insisted really. She'd refused, too fretful for what the money would signify. If or when she journeyed to Texas, she would pay her own way.

Her thoughts were interrupted by Hope. Her sister opened the door, a shocked expression on her face. She held a letter in her trembling hand.

Faith jumped to her feet, her heart thudding in her chest. "What is it?" she whispered.

"It's Grace," Hope said quietly. "She and Thomas are expecting a child."

And with that news, Faith made her decision. She'd go to Texas. Immediately, or as soon as she could purchase a train ticket. Over the course of the next few days she packed and repacked her things. She elected to take only a single valise. The notion of packing every one of her belongings into trunks and loading them onto the train seemed too permanent. If she arrived in Magnolia with all her possessions, Grace, and Thomas too, would see it as an admission she intended to stay for good.

That wouldn't do at all.

Instead, she packed a few simple dresses, not the fancy dresses she wore to Mrs. Caldicott's, but serviceable, nonetheless. She added a prettier one in case she and Grace could attend services at the church in Houston. She packed sturdy, but ladylike, boots, ones that she prayed would be suitable for the rough Texas terrain. With Mrs. Caldicott's money, she bought herself a few lacy, feminine undergarments. From Grace's letters, she surmised that Magnolia was uncivilized, overrun by men. She was certain they didn't have shops for ladies' apparel.

Mrs. Caldicott had given her several pairs of kid gloves and taught her on the proper glove etiquette. Since then, Faith never went outdoors without gloves. Indeed, she'd packed three pairs in her valise. And despite her misgivings about Thomas Bentley, she couldn't arrive in Magnolia without a gift for him and his boy.

She visited a haberdashery to buy them some gloves. Grace had written that "Thomas was pleasant looking and a few inches taller than Papa." With that in mind, she purchased a pair of large, finely-stitched gloves she hoped would fit a man of his stature. She also bought a smaller pair for Caleb.

Several days later, she stood in the train station with Hope and had to confess that she hadn't written Thomas to tell him she was on her way.

"You intend to surprise him?" Hope said, her eyes round as plums. "Is that wise?"

"Of course, it's sensible. I'm always sensible."

Faith wanted to remind her sister that she was, in fact, the sensible sister, the one who thought things through and made wise decisions. Not like Grace who wore her heart on her sleeve. Or Hope who was so stubborn she'd argue aloud with the characters in her beloved novels.

A cool breeze blew through the train station, carrying a gust of smoke past the girls. Faith turned away and covered her mouth with a handkerchief. Hope grimaced at the stench of smoldering coal.

"I worry about you traveling alone," Hope said. "But I want you to leave before the weather turns cold."

"You promise to come? Soon?"

"I will."

Faith didn't miss how slowly her sister replied. She would have liked to get a firm commitment from Hope, but the conductor yelled an "all aboard". There was no time for more talk. The two sisters embraced, said a tearful farewell, and Faith climbed up the steps of the train. She tried to keep the tears from falling as the train lurched from the platform. She waved to Hope, keeping her gaze fixed on her sister until she disappeared from view.

Chapter Six

Thomas

Thomas leaned against the porch railing and watched Caleb present his latest round of tricks he'd taught Buster. The dog, a youngster that appeared at the ranch last month, had been full of mischief at first.

Thomas threatened to run the animal off the ranch if he didn't stop chasing the chickens. He'd made the mistake of grousing about the dog around his son. Caleb promptly set about teaching the dog some manners, along with a few amusing tricks.

The wind rustled through the live oak trees surrounding the house. Spanish moss, hanging from the branches, swayed in the southerly breeze. Swallowtails swooped in the evening sky, catching the last of the late summer's mosquitoes.

Buster lay on the ground, doing his darnedest to remain perfectly still. His eyes were focused squarely on Caleb, standing a few paces away. When Caleb didn't move or speak, the dog couldn't help himself and thumped his tail.

"Dead dog, Buster."

The tail went still. Caleb made him wait a moment longer before praising him. The dog leapt up and bounded to the boy, an explosion of wriggles and happy barking.

"Not bad," Thomas said. "I'd like him to stay like that a little longer. Can he play dead all day? I think the chickens would approve of that trick, especially."

Caleb knelt beside the dog to pet him and give him a small crust of bread. "He can barely hold on for half a minute, and his tail hasn't learned to stay still for more than a few seconds. But he's doing better, don't you think?"

"I do, son. You've taught him some good manners. He's on his way to becoming a good ranch dog."

"Do you think Faith likes dogs?"

"Hope so. We've got six."

"I picture her as a lady who likes cats. She seems sort of prim and proper."

Thomas frowned. He wasn't sure how Caleb had come to that opinion, but he was probably right. The boy had an uncanny ability to judge people and animals correctly. Thomas must have mentioned something about Faith that led him to conclude she was prim and proper. If that was so, she was in for a surprise. Their house was simple. Primitive even.

Whenever Thomas wondered about Faith, he'd find himself using Grace as a sort of measuring stick. Grace was ladylike, to be sure, but she was happy to be outdoors and wasn't offended by a little dirt or a few ranch dogs milling around.

She seemed to like children too. When she arrived in Magnolia, she immediately took over care of her adopted daughter, Abigail. She'd always been sweet with Caleb, and the boy loved her. She often sewed new shirts and trousers for him. She'd greet him with a hug and pat the chair next to her asking him to sit a spell and chat. But she had a little one on the way, not to mention Abigail. Once the baby arrived, it was understandable her attention would diminish.

Caleb must have anticipated that too, and, for that reason, clung to the hope that Faith would care for him. The look in his son's eyes when he spoke of Faith always sent a jolt of pain through Thomas's heart. Thomas would rather suffer any injury than see his boy hurting. Caleb talked about writing Faith every so often but never did. He seemed worried that he might offend her or write something that would make her not want to come.

Thomas got the strong feeling she had second thoughts, but it wasn't on account of Caleb. It was on account of him. He gritted his teeth. Who needed that sort of woman around?

Caleb stopped petting the dog, stood up and showed Thomas how Buster could shake paws, fetch a stick, drop it at Caleb's feet, and go to his bed on the porch.

After that, Lucas called them to dinner. Caleb groaned at the smell of burned eggs. He kicked off his boots and trudged to the kitchen, grumbling all the way.

Thomas wasn't too keen on another dinner of scrambled eggs either. They'd had cooks in the past, but none of the women ever stayed long. They were all older and none relished working for a pair of set-in-their-way bachelors and a boy who avoided regular baths.

Lucas set the fry pan on the table, eggs still sizzling, adding another scorch mark to the worn wood.

"You're wrecking the table, Uncle Lucas," Caleb muttered.

"It's called adding character," Lucas argued. "Anyone can have a table without history. Just run down to the sawmill and order a brand-new one."

"When I grow up, I'm not having tables with history. I'm getting everything new. And I'm getting married as soon as I'm of age."

Lucas snorted. He cut a slice of bread from a loaf Mrs. Patchwell had baked last week. He tossed it across the table, aiming for Caleb's plate, but missing. The slice landed half on the plate, half on the table. Caleb scowled as he studied the bread and flicked off a few stray pieces of grit.

Thomas ladled a heap of scorched eggs on Caleb's plate and served himself. When Lucas tossed the slice of bread on his plate, it landed squarely in the middle. Thomas squinted at the bread.

"What?" Lucas barked.

Thomas shrugged. "Nothing, just a little mold."

Caleb gagged and stared at horror at his plate. "Didn't you check before you sliced it?"

Lucas held up the loaf for Caleb's inspection. "Course I did. I already cut off the biggest spots."

He turned the loaf around as proof of his efforts. Chunks of bread had been carved off the sides and bottom. Caleb made a gagging noise again, covering his mouth with his hand.

"You see," Lucas growled. "This is what happens after we eat at Matt and Grace's. Everyone gets their nose out of joint by a little speck of mold."

"That's hardly a speck," Thomas muttered. "That bread looks like it's got a bad case of pocks."

Caleb clutched his stomach. "Quit saying that. I'm gonna be sick."

Lucas sat down and dug into his eggs with a vengeance. He glared at Caleb, but mostly at Thomas, because he blamed his brother anytime he ate at Matt's and Grace's home. Never mind that he ate there just as often.

"Pretty soon you'll have a red-headed wife that'll treat you like royalty," Lucas said, his eyes flashing. "I'll live here by myself and enjoy eating dinner without a bunch of complainers."

Caleb dropped his hands from his mid-section. He poked at his dinner with his fork but finding that his fork wasn't clean enough for his liking, wiped it on his pants. He took a tentative bite of eggs and chewed slowly. Thomas heard the unmistakable crunch of eggshells, but Caleb didn't notice or didn't care enough to grumble.

Thomas tried to imagine a day when he'd sit down to a civilized dinner, one cooked by a wife. If that day ever came to pass, he and Caleb wouldn't live here with Lucas. They'd take the other house on the Bentley ranch. The house his brother John lived in before he died of a snake bite.

It was a fair bit more refined than this place, Thomas had to admit. Mrs. Patchwell called his and Lucas's home "a bear den with furniture". Her words always made him laugh. He never denied the truth behind her words. If he ever married again, he'd move his family to John's home, and enjoy the old family homestead.

The house sat amidst a grove of oaks, shuttered, the furnishings covered in sheets, the silent rooms waiting to be filled with a happy family. Someday. It was understood that the next brother to marry would inherit the house. If he were lucky, the home would belong to him and Caleb.

Lucas's grumbling drew him from his thoughts. "My cooking doesn't come close to Mrs. Patchwell's or Grace's but at least it's something."

"It needs a woman's touch," Caleb said, ignoring Lucas's frown. "I thought you were writing Grace's sister."

"I was," Lucas replied. "Pretty sure she's not interested. Which is fine by me. I wasn't sure I was interested in the first place. I only wrote her because Grace gave me that look."

Both Caleb and Thomas nodded.

"I know just which look you mean," Caleb said. He tilted his head and gazed at his uncle, wide-eyed, his mouth slightly pursed. He added a long, unhappy sigh. "Is that it?"

"Exactly that," Thomas said.

Lucas nodded. "Except when she's really bent on getting her way, she'll get a little teary-eyed. Females seem to know that if they add tears, it'll clinch the deal."

Thomas chuckled. Grace could talk any of them into anything. She had Matt wrapped around her pinky. It wasn't often she pressed to get her way. She wasn't manipulative, not like some women. No, she picked her battles, and they were usually when she wanted the Bentley men to take some care, to be safe.

She'd asked Lucas and Thomas to write to her sisters too, but in truth it hadn't been much of a sacrifice. Both Lucas and Thomas esteemed Grace. They admired her kindness, and gentle ways. She cared for Abigail like the girl was her own, and ever since she'd arrived, the small girl had blossomed. When she first asked them to write her sisters, they'd agreed happily because both Lucas and Thomas assumed the women were amenable.

They weren't.

"You don't think Hope wants to come to Magnolia?" Thomas asked.

Lucas shrugged. "She's being ornery. I don't think she's like Grace at all. Maybe because she's the baby of the family. Spoiled probably. I seen that happen before."

Caleb knit his brow. "But aren't you the baby of the family?"

Lucas shook his head. "Eat your dinner, Caleb."

Caleb made a face and muttered something about dinner always being the same as breakfast.

Thomas had intended to talk to his brother about the conversation he'd had with Baron Calhoun last week. He'd hardly thought about the robbery in Fort Worth, but Baron had sent him a note that he'd heard the Grimes sister had definite plans to travel to Magnolia in the next few days. Thomas wanted to ask Lucas to help watch the passengers who arrived at the train station.

His thoughts went back to Faith. It had been three weeks since she'd written and his hope of courting her faded a little more each day. Maybe Lucas was right. Maybe the two sisters were nothing like Grace. The notion that Hope and Faith might be quite different troubled him. He ate his eggs and stale bread, hardly noticing the taste.

Chapter Seven

Faith

The train ride seemed interminable. When Faith imagined traveling to Texas, she'd envisioned a romantic idea that she'd pass the time admiring the lovely landscape. She thought the train would provide meals and such. Instead, she was forced to get off the train when it stopped and search for something to eat amongst the food sellers in the train stations.

Each stop was a new venture. On the second day, she'd only been able to procure apples. So the following day, she was desperate for anything other than apples. Fortunately, she'd managed to find hot beef sandwiches. To her mortification, she ate three, taking a long nap afterwards, resting against her valise.

For the rest of the trip, Faith made certain to buy more food than she thought she'd need. She tucked the morsels away in her valise, feeling a little like a squirrel preparing for winter. Several times she found she had more than she needed and shared her stores with some of the other passengers, ladies of course. Faith avoided the male passengers entirely.

She was grateful for the companionship of female passengers. They tended to sit together, seeking each other out amidst the throngs of travelers. For much of the journey west, she traveled with an older woman and her two daughters. The trio journeyed to Texas to visit the woman's sister. Faith was sorry to say goodbye to them in Fort Worth.

Amid the bustle of the town, a woman made her way onto the train, taking one of the empty seats across from Faith. She was elegant, dressed in a lovely frock, her hair swept up in a tidy chignon. The woman was friendly, explaining that Fort Worth's nickname was "Cowtown".

"My name's Priscilla," the woman said, offering a gloved hand.

"My name's Faith. Pleased to meet you."

Faith stared at the sights outside the window as the train pulled out of the station. She glimpsed an enormous cloud of dust on the horizon, so thick that it darkened the sun. A feeling of unease grew inside her. Was it a dust storm? She'd read about them and prayed they wouldn't have to pass through the ominous mass.

"You look a mite worried, Faith. You needn't be. That's likely a herd of longhorns, headed for Kansas City."

Faith gave the woman an embarrassed smile. "I admit I was a little concerned."

"Fort Worth is part of the Chisholm Trail. Texas ranchers send their cattle up to Kansas City, to the railhead, and from there, the animals are loaded on trains. Texas beef is famous, you might say."

The woman spoke with obvious pride.

Faith studied the billowing dust, marveling at the size of the cloud, and tried to imagine the enormous herd of cattle. What did Thomas and his brothers do with their cattle? A surge of excitement gripped her. Maybe she could travel with them as they made their way north. From the safety of her imagination, she indulged in the absurd notion. She saw herself astride a horse or driving a wagon. She'd never done anything of the kind, but the thrill of possibility swept her imagination away.

She wasn't one to indulge in dreams of adventure, but the wide-open spaces invited her mind to dream – just a small one, of course. Nothing foolhardy.

Thomas had pressed her for a firm commitment to marry him. He'd wanted to send a proxy, but she'd refused, saying she wanted to have a proper marriage. In truth, she'd wanted to ascertain that Grace was well. If she was satisfied that her sister was happily married, she'd consider Thomas's offer of matrimony.

A plan formed in her mind. He was eager to marry. She knew that. Perhaps she could bargain with him. She could agree to marry him, if he would take her on a cattle drive. The idea made her smile inwardly even though she knew she could barely manage a simple conversation with a stranger, much less negotiate some outlandish deal.

Priscilla didn't provide the same companionship as the prior seatmates. She seemed more interested in her book than chitchat. Faith squinted trying to read the title of the book that had so intrigued the woman. She couldn't make out the title but saw that the author was Jane Austen.

Her sister, Hope, would have approved of the woman's excellent choice. Jane Austen wasn't one of Faith's favorites, but it made her happy to remember the way Hope smiled or swooned when she read any of her works. She had several well-loved volumes stacked by her bedside at any given time.

Faith let her mind return to romantic notions of a cattle drive. She pictured the wide-open landscape they'd ride through during the day, and the star-studded sky they'd sleep under at night. They'd cook their food over an open fire. She imagined sitting around a campfire.

Now she wished she'd asked Thomas more about his family's ranch, and the cattle they raised. She was so caught up in the thoughts swirling in her mind, she hardly noticed the train slowing as they approached a small depot.

Priscilla made a small sound of dismay.

"Are you all right?" Faith asked.

Her companion nodded. "You see those men out there? They're Texas Rangers."

Faith followed her gaze to see a group of men on horseback. This was the first time she'd seen a cowboy up close. The men wore jeans and leather chaps, boots with spurs. Their hard expressions sent a shiver up her spine.

"They look fearsome," she whispered.

"They are. Most of them are as rough as the criminals they pursue."

"My word," Faith said, drawing back from the window.

"They can be terrible men, acting like judge, jury and executioner in one fell swoop. If they find me here..."

Faith stared in disbelief. The woman, elegantly dressed and obviously refined, seemed so far removed from any sort of criminal element. And yet, her face colored with distress.

"It's not me," Priscilla stammered. "It's my brothers. If they catch me, I won't be able to travel to Magnolia."

Faith gasped. "I'm traveling to Magnolia."

Priscilla drew a sharp breath. "You don't say!"

Faith pointed to her valise and the ticket the agent had given her in Boston. "You see? Magnolia, Texas."

"This is uncanny! Perhaps I could impose upon you to..." She covered her mouth with her gloved hand. "No. I couldn't possibly. How could I ask a stranger to take medicine to a sick child?"

Two of the men, grim-faced and resolute, approached the train. They spoke to the conductor who didn't seem to want to let them board. The men promptly took out their pistols and threatened the man with words Faith couldn't hear, but she could certainly understand.

"My word," she breathed, wondering if she were dreaming.

"I suppose my nephew won't get the medicine he so desperately needs," Priscilla said tearfully. "I'll need to depart the train before they find me."

"I'll take the medicine," Faith blurted. "Leave it with me."

Priscilla let out a cry of anguished relief. "Bless you, Faith. You're a true angel." Without another word, she shoved a bag under Faith's seat. "My brother's name is Billy Grimes. He might be at the station. If not, you can leave the bag with the station master."

"I'll find him. Don't you worry. What's your nephew's name?"

"Um... pardon me?"

"Your nephew, the boy who needs the medicine. What's his name?"

Priscilla looked confused for a moment and Faith felt badly for asking the woman questions when she was clearly distressed. Outside, the two Rangers who wanted to board the train shouted at the conductor. A few of the other Rangers had dismounted and joined them to help convince the hapless conductor. Faith wondered if she might witness some violence.

"His name is..." Priscilla seemed to be momentarily overcome by the shouting outside their window.

Faith was about to dismiss the question and tell the woman that she should leave the train to escape the rough men on the platform. Her heart went out to the poor woman.

"It's Fitzwilliam," Priscilla said, with a resolute expression.

"Fitzwilliam Grimes. That should be easy to remember. Rest assured, I'll be sure to get the medicine to the dear boy."

The men no longer stood on the platform, which meant they had to be inside the train. The conductor sat on the ground, looking dazed, a knot forming on his brow. Faith drew a sharp breath.

"You'd best go, Priscilla. Save yourself from those terrible men."

Priscilla gave a breathless laugh. "Thank you, Faith. I appreciate you more than I could ever say."

With that she was gone, a whirl of petticoats vanishing down the narrow train aisle. Outside, the conductor got to his feet. He swayed. He blinked, seemingly confused as to where he was. Priscilla strode across the platform without so much as a glance in Faith's direction. With a purposeful stride, she stepped into the train station, just as the Rangers arrived in the doorway of Faith's train car.

Faith patted the bag, feeling a surge of determination. Normally she'd fret if a man even looked her direction, but a child needed medicine. The responsibility gave her a sense of tremendous purpose. A child waited for her in Magnolia. And she would rise to the cause.

Mrs. Caldicott's words echoed in her mind.

You're braver than you know...

The Rangers surveyed the passengers with a grim and determined air about them. Despite Faith's distaste for rough men, particularly rough lawmen, she had to admit the three Rangers made an impression.

Their faces were tanned, burnished from years of riding under a hot, unforgiving Texas sun. Each had a scruff of a beard. All three looked dusty and gritty and ready to mete out some primitive code of justice. Faith pressed against her seat.

The movement attracted the attention of the lead man. He narrowed his eyes and folded his arms across his chest. When he spoke, it was in a loud, booming voice that commanded respect. "There are two passengers heading to Magnolia."

No one moved. At first. Faith held her breath, as she slowly raised her hand.

The Ranger closed the distance between them, stopping a few paces away as he swiped the hat from his head. He nodded, a gesture that seemed respectful, but gave her no sense of relief or confidence.

"Ma'am," he rasped. "May I ask what your business is in Magnolia?"

"I'm going to see my sister," Faith said, her voice trembling.

He squinted as if the notion of visiting one's sister implied guilt for some horrible transgression.

"Also..." Faith swallowed hard. "I'm to meet my husband-to-be."

It was a slight overstatement, but Faith thought it might strengthen her argument.

He knit his brow, letting his gaze slowly travel down her face and lower as he appraised the rest of her. A burn of mortification scorched her. The nerve. The utter disrespect for a single, vulnerable woman. Priscilla had been right about the uncouth nature of the Texas lawmen. If anything, she'd understated the point. For a moment, Faith forgot entirely about her task of delivering medicine to poor Fitzwilliam Grimes.

"Who are you marrying?" the man asked.

"Thomas Bentley."

The man's jaw dropped. His eyes grew round. For a moment, he just stared in disbelief. Finally, recovering his senses, he managed a response. "Thomas Bentley... you don't say. I never thought I'd see the day he'd take another wife."

The car didn't hold many passengers, only a handful of people waiting for the train to be on its way. All of them craned their necks to look at her. Her face burned. She disliked the lawman more with each passing moment, resenting both his questions and the clear amusement he found in her mention of Thomas. How could a Texas Ranger in Fort Worth know Thomas Bentley of Magnolia?

Whatever his reason for chuckling at her answer, he seemed satisfied that she wasn't the person he was looking for. Giving her a respectful nod, he wished her good day and continued to make his way through the train. When he left the train car, Faith leaned down and patted Priscilla's bag to reassure herself that it was safe and sound.

Faith waited, her heart hammering against her ribs. Everything felt like some sort of dream. She could hardly believe she'd just stood up for herself, to a roughhewn, Texas lawman! Wouldn't her sisters be amazed. And Mrs. Caldicott too. She'd write her first thing to tell her about the Rangers, and the herd of cattle, and especially the details of delivering medicine to poor Fitzwilliam Grimes.

She could feel the curious gazes of the other passengers fixed upon her. She avoided their eyes, keeping her back to them as she stared out the window. Petrified that the men would return, she scarcely dared to breath. A short while later, she saw the men standing on the platform. Dusk gathered, silhouetting the men's powerful figures against the evening sky. The whistle blew, and the train pulled away from the station of Fort Worth.

Chapter Eight

Thomas

The warmth of the afternoon sun made Thomas yawn. Or perhaps the tired feeling came from the boredom of waiting around the Magnolia train depot. The platform was deserted. Usually there were a few people milling around, but not today.

A wave of resentment came over Thomas. Next time he saw Baron Calhoun, he'd tell the man to wait for the Grimes sister himself. Baron seemed so dead certain she was coming, but Thomas wasn't so sure. This marked his fifth day waiting for the woman, and his patience wore thin. He had other things to do.

Often months would go by without having to don his sheriff's badge. That suited him just fine. He liked the work, felt it was a privilege to serve the citizens of Magnolia, but he didn't necessarily enjoy all the tasks that needed doing. Like waiting around an empty train platform.

In the years he'd worked as a sheriff, he'd had plenty of tasks that made the job worthwhile. Like when two small children had wandered off from their home and gotten lost in the thick, mesquite brushlands. He'd searched for days, combing the rough arroyos around Magnolia, camping in the hills at night. He'd been driven to find them. When he'd discovered them, sheltering in a small cave, and returned them to their frantic parents, he'd felt a sense of satisfaction that ranching never offered.

There were times that tested his patience, though. Like waiting for some woman who might or might not arrive on a train. That morning he'd had other mundane business to attend to when he'd hauled Bing Giddings to jail for disorderly conduct. The man had gotten drunk and tried to start a fight with his barber. Never a good idea to cuss a man holding a blade, but that was Bing for you.

Bing Giddings was known around Magnolia as a fine lawyer. As a young man, he'd traveled to the East Coast to attend law school. Normally, he was a bright, law-abiding citizen, except for when the anniversary of his wife's death rolled around.

For a month, he'd stagger around town, drinking and carrying on, until he got tired of waking up with a sore head, locked up in jail. Then he'd get back on the straight and narrow and stay there for the better part of a year. Come September, though, he'd start moping and go through the whole rigamarole all over again.

Thomas had avoided telling Faith that he worked as a sheriff. Grace had urged him to write her a letter to explain his side job. He'd intended to, but never gotten around to it. The truth was that he didn't want to give Faith another reason to stay in Boston. He was certain she'd put a little black mark next to his name if she knew he often had to collar rough criminals. The mark would probably be one of many.

He gritted his teeth as he recalled her last letter. She'd explained that she had to put off her trip to Texas "indefinitely" since her employer, Mrs. Caldicott, needed her. He wanted to write back to say that he needed her too. His pride kept him from putting the words on paper.

Let her take her time. She'd come around when Grace had her baby. He was sure of the strong sisterly bond. Both Hope and Faith would want to see their niece or nephew when the time came.

His attention was drawn to an approaching figure. Baron Calhoun strode across the platform, looking pleased as could be. His grin irritated Thomas for some reason.

"Good to see you, Thomas," he said, offering a handshake.

"You look like you've gotten some good news."

Baron shook his head. "I do?"

"Maybe it's just wishful thinking. Here I was hoping you'd found the Grimes brothers along with the stolen loot."

Baron shoved his hands in his pockets, his grin widening. "I believe that's your job, Sheriff."

"I'm about run out of patience, Calhoun. I've wasted too much daylight on your problem. If she doesn't show up today, you'll need to hire a man to stand here."

"She's coming," Baron said cheerfully. "I'm sure of it."

Thomas didn't ask how Baron was so darned sure of anything. The man owned half the town. If there was something to be found out, he had any number of people he could ask.

"Maybe you ought to be sheriff," Thomas grumbled.

Off in the distance, a train whistle blew.

Baron chuckled. "I don't want to be sheriff. I'm too mean-spirited."

Thomas couldn't help but smile. "Being a little mean-spirited comes with the territory. After you've spent a little time with criminals, it's second-nature."

"I know about all that. I spent a few years as a bounty hunter."

Thomas regarded Baron with surprise. Baron Calhoun was a self-made man, one who made a fortune buying and selling land. He liked money, almost more than anything in the world. All that had changed when he'd married, of course. Now he was a love-sick fool. Despite the man's height and obvious strength, it was hard to imagine him collaring criminals.

"I've come to the train station to make sure you're mean-spirited enough, Thomas. You've never dealt with a female crook. I'm not certain you're prepared to do what's needed."

Thomas scowled. "I know how to do my job, Calhoun."

"From what I've heard, you're having trouble managing your bride-to-be."

The train whistled again, closer now.

"Aren't you curious how I know?" Baron asked.

Thomas didn't care for the question, or the way Baron's eyes sparked with amusement.

"I'm guessing you ran into Caleb, or Lucas, and they gave you an earful," Thomas growled.

"Caleb! The boy's counting the days. Or he'd like to be counting the days. If only Miss O'Brian would agree to come."

"And you're a gossiping old-"

The train's whistle cut off the rest of Thomas's words as it rolled around the bend in the track. The ground rumbled beneath his feet as it chugged into the station. Smoke billowed from the stack and carried on the north wind, drifting away from the station.

Thomas pushed off the wall and moved closer. Few people waited for the train, making today's work easier. If the Grimes woman was on the train, she wouldn't be able to get lost in the crowd. The conductor jumped from the train as it ground to a halt. He grabbed a wooden step from the platform and set it in front of the doorway. Only a single passenger waited to disembark, and to Thomas's shock, the passenger was a woman.

Baron came to his side. "You see, sheriff? I was right."

The woman wore a bonnet, which covered her hair so well, it was impossible to see what color it was. She shaded her eyes to look around, searching the platform.

"I thought you said she was an older woman," Thomas said.

"She is," Baron insisted, frowning as he studied the woman in question.

"Maybe you got the wrong information."

"I never get the wrong information."

Thomas kept his gaze fixed on the woman. "That's why you ought to be sheriff."

The conductor spoke with the woman, but Thomas could hear nothing over the noise of the locomotive. The man pointed towards him and Baron. The woman's eyes widened, and she shook her head. Thomas stared, struck by her lovely face. She was fair, petite, and dressed in a simple gown that accentuated her narrow waist. He moved towards her without any conscious thought, drawn inexplicably.

The conductor ushered her across the platform. "Why are you afraid of Rangers, miss?"

"I simply don't wish to run into one of them. I've been told they're rough-mannered, and I saw with my own eyes their treatment of one of the conductors in Fort Worth."

The conductor shrugged. "Well, miss, this here is the sheriff. He can help you find the person you're looking for."

The young woman bit her lip as she looked up at Thomas. She paled and swallowed hard. The conductor tipped his hat and hurried away to help unload crates and whatnot from steerage.

“You looking for somebody, miss?” Thomas asked. His voice was gruffer than usual, probably because he felt more than just a glimmer of jealousy. He wasn’t sure what that was about. Normally he ignored pretty, young women, but he had to admit that he hoped she wasn’t looking for a sweetheart.

“I am looking for someone,” she said.

Her voice was so soft, he had to guess at her reply. He gestured to the train station and ushered her away from the rumble of the locomotive. Baron followed, despite the hard look Thomas gave him. They stepped inside the station. Baron closed the door behind them.

She held back, trying to keep her distance from him and Baron. The two were both a few inches over six foot and probably their sheer size intimidated her.

“You’re the sheriff?” she asked, speaking softly.

The conductor had already explained that, but she must not have given his words much credence.

“He is,” Baron said. “I’m Baron Calhoun. Owner of the Magnolia Bank and Trust.” He softened his tone. “At your service.”

“My name is Faith O’Brian.”

Thomas stared at her, wondering if his mind played tricks on him. Had this trembling woman just claimed to be Faith? His Faith? Impossible. He was vaguely aware of Baron giving a huff of astonishment. The woman’s gaze went back and forth between the two men as if trying to fathom why they were so surprised. Their response seemed to embolden her slightly.

She took a tentative step forward. “I’m looking for the Grimes family.” She lifted a small satchel. “I have an important delivery for Fitzwilliam Grimes.”

Chapter Nine

Faith

Both men gaped at her. When they recovered their senses, the sheriff led her to his office, a dusty, squat building near the train station. He claimed that they needed to have a little chat. She couldn't imagine why her delivery would spark such a stir and wondered if she should simply request assistance to the Bentley Ranch. Once she saw Grace, she could ask her sister's help with her task.

Why had she come to Texas without telling anyone? Her plan seemed foolhardy now. Reckless. She tried to set her worries aside. If she concentrated on the matter at hand, she felt what had to be confidence. She needed to cling to that small shred of self-assurance.

"How do you know the Grimes family, Miss O'Brian?" the sheriff asked.

The man leaned against his desk, his legs crossed at the ankle, regarding her with a mix of amusement and disbelief. The other man, the fellow who said he was a banker, stood beside him, with a similar expression on his face.

"What concern is it of yours?" she asked. "Is it a crime to know the family?"

"Not at all," the sheriff replied. His voice, she had to admit, was pleasant. Deep and resonant, with a drawl that might have made her smile if she hadn't thought he was mocking her.

"It's just a friendly question."

Something stirred in the cell behind her, startling her. A crash followed by a groan of pain. She turned to find a cell behind her. From the shadows, a man appeared. Faith couldn't help the small cry of dismay that fell from her lips. The man staggered to the door and squinted at her. He wore a rumpled shirt, trousers and a single boot. On his other foot he wore a sock that needed darning. His big toe poked out a hole.

"Hey, sheriff," the man rasped. "You got any more coffee?"

The prisoner spoke without taking his gaze from her, staring at her as if not quite believing his eyes, and a few swallows of coffee would clear up his confusion.

Without a word, the sheriff ambled to a black, pot-bellied stove and poured a cup of coffee into a tin cup. He opened a small jar, dropped two sugar cubes into the coffee and stirred it with a fork. After he gave the coffee to the prisoner, he returned to his spot by the desk.

"Now, where were we?" the man asked. "Ah, how do you know the Grimes family? Are you a friend of theirs?"

The prisoner choked on his coffee. "Her? Doubtful."

"Drink your coffee, Bing," the sheriff said.

The prisoner, Bing, grunted and returned to his cot. "Fine. I know when I'm not wanted."

"I'm not friends with them, but I'm acquainted with their sister. Priscilla. She asked me to deliver this bag to them."

"They ain't around," Bing offered. "They up and left last week."

"What?" Mr. Calhoun demanded, clearly outraged. "Where did you hear that?"

"I knocked back a few drinks with them a week ago." Bing frowned. "Or was it two weeks ago? I'm their lawyer."

Mr. Calhoun crossed his arms over his chest. "Where'd they go?"

Bing looked affronted. "Now, Baron, you know I can't discuss my clients with you."

Faith rubbed her forehead, wondering what sort of people lived in the town of Magnolia. "Is Fitzwilliam still here?"

When neither the sheriff nor the banker responded, she turned her attention to the prisoner.

"Ma'am?" he asked.

"Fitzwilliam Grimes. The boy. Did he leave as well?"

The man stared for a long moment and then threw his head back with a round of raucous laughter. His amusement quickly gave way to a yelp of pain when he sloshed coffee on his leg. After his pain subsided, he chuckled and wiped tears from his eyes. "There's no Fitzwilliam, ma'am."

"Priscilla said the boy needed medicine, though." Faith glanced down at the bag on her lap.

"I can tell you what's in that bag," Mr. Calhoun said with all the certainty in the world.

Something about his expression told her he wasn't going to say the bag contained medicine, and she was beginning to think he'd be right. She shook her head, unsure what to say.

Mr. Calhoun came to her side and held out his hand. "I believe your bag contains a number of gold coins. Coins stolen from my bank in Fort Worth."

He smiled at her in a way that made her think he might be a kind man. The sheriff, on the other hand, made her nervous. Slowly, she handed him the bag, her thoughts spinning wildly. Gold coins?

She hiccupped and covered her mouth with her hand. Dear Lord, she prayed.

Please don't let me fall apart. Not now.

Mr. Calhoun reached into the bag and took out gold coins, one by one, gently setting them on the desk. They shone with a brilliance that made her forget for a moment that she'd transported stolen property. They were beautiful. She knew without a doubt they were worth a small fortune.

He set the bag aside and studied the coins, checking to see if all was accounted for. She hoped desperately there weren't any missing. What would happen if he claimed some were in fact missing? Would they think she had taken them?

The sheriff, meanwhile, regarded her with a widening smile. His teeth were white, a stark contrast to his tanned skin. He was handsome in a rough, dangerous sort of way. Coaxing air into her lungs, she did her best to remain calm. She'd done nothing, she assured herself. They couldn't fault her for trying to help another person, for being a good Samaritan.

Surely.

"What's that you got there?" Bing asked, returning to the door of his cell.

Mr. Calhoun took one of the coins from the desk and showed it to the prisoner.

The man whistled. "That's a Spanish doubloon."

"It is," Mr. Calhoun replied. "You can see why I was anxious to get the coins back in my possession, I'm sure."

"Those Grimes boys told me they'd pay their bill with Spanish gold," Bing mused. "I told them I preferred cash. Now they're gone, and I don't have either."

"It's your own fault, Bing," the sheriff said. "If I've told you once, I've told you a hundred times. You shouldn't consort with criminals."

With that, both Mr. Calhoun and the sheriff turned their attention to Faith. They studied her as if they thought she was the very sort of criminal Bing should avoid. She swallowed hard, trying to dislodge the lump in her throat. It didn't help. Nothing helped. She felt herself wither under their scrutiny. How had things gone so terribly wrong?

"I think I'm having a bad dream," she whispered.

"Now, don't you fret, Miss O'Brian," Mr. Calhoun said. "I would never press charges against a young lady who had unwittingly helped a bank robber. Would you, sheriff?"

The two men chuckled at the notion. Even Bing seemed to think the idea amusing. What sort of place was Magnolia, she wondered again. And how soon could she leave?

"I'll have to give it some thought," the sheriff said. "I wouldn't care to testify against Miss O'Brian. Seeing as I hoped to propose to her one day."

Faith hiccupped again. This time she was too stunned to cover her mouth or wish the hiccups away. "I beg your pardon?"

"You know? Propose. Get down on bended knee to the woman I've been writing to for four months."

She stared in horror. Could it be? Was this Thomas Bentley? "Four months," she breathed.

"That's right. Only lately it seems that my fiancée can't bother to write me back, maybe because she's too busy planning her next heist."

Merciful heavens. This could not be happening. It couldn't be possible.

Bing snorted. "You don't say. I never thought I'd see the day that Thomas Bentley would marry again."

Faith's hand flew to her mouth, but not fast enough to hold back a panicked shriek. She gaped. The man before her was Thomas Bentley. Now she was certain that she was caught in the middle of a terrible nightmare. She stared at him, taking in the details of his height and work-toughened and muscular form. Amidst her utter panic, she noticed he was handsome, if it weren't for that dratted smirk.

"That was what I hoped for," Thomas said. "To marry again. I hadn't imagined my girl would run with such a dangerous crowd." He shook his head. "The Grimes family is *legendary*."

"You can't be serious," Faith whispered. "You're the last man on earth I want to marry."

Thomas set his hand on his heart and winced, mocking her.

"I can tell you one good legal reason to marry," Bing said.

"I'd like to know," Mr. Calhoun said. "I think it would be grand if the sheriff settled down."

"I think I can help," Bing said. "And I'll give you my advice pro bono."

The three men spoke as if she weren't in the room. She wanted to wave her hands and shout at the men, but her throat was too tight to say a peep. Despite a deep sense of outrage, she found herself waiting to hear Bing's reason for her to marry Thomas. Not that it mattered. As soon as she was done here, she'd run from the musty office and find a way to get to Grace and Matt's home.

"Well," Bing said, rubbing his scruffy jaw. "Here's the thing of it. There's a certain law called spousal privilege."

"Right," Thomas said. "I think I've heard of that."

The grin playing on his mouth told her that he knew good and well what spousal privilege was.

"A wife can't testify against her husband, and vice versa." Bing began pacing along the front of his cell, his gait lopsided by the missing boot. "See, the court doesn't want to give a man and wife reason to argue. They view them as one person."

"Well, isn't that nice," Thomas drawled. "A man and wife become one person. Imagine that. Just what I was proposing all along."

Faith had heard enough. She got to her feet, a little unsteadily, and gave Thomas a hard look, as forceful a glare as she'd ever mustered. Part of the effect was probably diminished by another dratted hiccup. "Would you kindly take me to my sister's home?"

"Certainly," Thomas said good-naturedly.

That had been a little easier than she'd imagined. "Thank you."

"I'm afraid that once we get there, I'll have to put you under house arrest."

Mr. Calhoun and Bing laughed heartily at Thomas's remark. Faith was certain she'd never been so angry in all her life. She was angry at the woman on the train, Priscilla, if that was even her name. She was angry with the three men here in the sheriff's office, especially the one wearing the sheriff star. Mostly she was angry with herself for being so foolish.

The only good thing about the charade she'd been forced to endure was that it made her so furious it lessened the severity of her hiccups.

A little.

Chapter Ten

Thomas

Baron offered to send a buckboard over to the jail, so Thomas could take Grace out to the Bentley Ranch. Thomas had accepted. While he waited for the wagon, he sent Bing on his way, with a word of warning about staying out of trouble.

Whenever Bing was having one of his grieving spells, he'd leave the jail and head to the nearest saloon. With Faith standing on the steps of the jail, he seemed to think better of his usual routine. Instead of walking in the direction of the saloon, he trudged off to the barber shop. He looked a sight. Disheveled. Walking unevenly because of his missing boot, and still a little unsteady on his feet.

"Don't cuss at Melvin," Thomas called. "He's the only barber in Magnolia. Not to mention he owns a collection of razors."

Bing waved off his words.

"I mean it, Bing. If I gotta come back to town because of your carrying on, I'll lock you up and throw away the key."

Bing glanced over his shoulder, giving Faith a sheepish look before scowling at Thomas. "I'm just getting my boot back. Then I'm heading home. I got court in a couple of days. I won't cuss him or anyone. Nice to have made your acquaintance, ma'am."

Faith nodded and gave him a half-hearted wave. She still looked a little stunned, and kept her distance from him, standing at the far end of the porch beside her tattered valise.

When the livery man delivered the buckboard, Thomas frowned. They'd hitched it to a team of mules. Thomas helped Faith up. He felt her flinch under his touch, but she didn't protest. He climbed up beside her and snapped the reins. He stole a glance at her, noting the edge of coppery hair peeking out from her bonnet. He hadn't noticed it before and yearned to see what she looked like without her hat. And just like that, he pondered what she'd look like with her hair hanging loose.

He knew the notion would scandalize her and she'd be even more indignant.

"You comfortable there, Miss O'Brian?"

She kept her gaze fixed straight in front of her, too furious to even look his way. "Yes, thank you."

"If I'd known you were coming to town, I would have made plans to squire you around in something finer than a buckboard and a team of ornery mules."

She said nothing.

"What do you think of Texas so far?"

With a slight shake of her head, she dismissed his question as not worthy of a response.

They drove a little further and soon were away from the dust and din of Magnolia. The road traveled along a pretty stretch of countryside and he was gratified when she took in the views. Her shoulders relaxed a little.

"I'm sure Grace will be over the moon to see you," he said.

Her expression softened. Her lips tilted slightly into a hint of what he imagined could be a lovely smile. Thomas felt his heart miss a beat. Trying not to stare, but unable to look away, he was astonished at the transformation the smile brought about. From the first moment he laid eyes on her, he'd been struck by her beauty, but her smile stole his breath.

"I've missed her." She spoke so softly, he might not have heard her words had he not glanced her direction. Her pretty smile faded. She bit her lip with a nervous apprehension and added, "so very much."

She'd barely spoken, but he could see that her words cost her. She grew pale and wrung her hands with a fretfulness that tugged at his heart. In the sheriff's office, she'd faced him with a confidence that bordered on sass. That spirit was gone now. Perhaps it was his fault for teasing her about arrest and whatnot. When he spoke with Gracie, he'd ask her how to make it up to Faith.

"Faith, I'm very glad you're here."

She blushed but said no more for the rest of the trip to the ranch. When they rounded the bend in the road, Matt and Grace's home appeared. Thomas smiled, imagining Grace's joy when she found out he'd brought her sister. What a grand surprise for all of them.

"That's their home," he said. "Your sister made it a home when she took in Abigail and married my brother. See the pretty flowers in front? She planted them, along with Abigail and my son Caleb."

Faith's smile returned as she took in the details of Matt and Grace's house.

"I imagined she'd be outside, but maybe she's resting," he said.

He drove the wagon closer and stopped at the hitching post. The dogs ran to greet them, barking and wagging their tails, but still no one appeared. Not even Mrs. Patchwell.

As he set the brake, a ranch hand emerged from the horse barn. He waved and ambled over, eyeing Faith with a curious expression. He took off his hat and nodded.

"Afternoon," Thomas said.

"Afternoon, sir. Ma'am."

"Where's everybody?"

"The little girl got to feeling poorly."

"Abigail?"

"Yes, sir. They took her to see the doc."

"In Magnolia?"

"No, sir, Houston." He scratched the back of his neck and frowned. "I believe that's what they said. They left at first light. The four of them."

"Mrs. Patchwell too?"

"Yes, sir. She insisted."

Thomas glanced at the empty house, considering what to do. "I've brought Mrs. Bentley's sister from town."

The man's brows shot up with surprise. Thomas wanted to shield her from his curiosity and could only imagine the rest of the cowboys appraising Faith.

He expected her to look terrified, but to his surprise, she spoke to the ranch hand.

"I don't suppose you know when they'll return, do you?"

"No, ma'am."

Thomas dismissed the man, sending him back to his chores. "I can't leave you here. Not alone. The ranch hands are a rough bunch and every so often they get a little out of hand."

"Out of hand?" she asked.

"Especially when the boss is away. They're likely planning a shindig right now."

"A shindig..."

Thomas wasn't sure if she knew what a shindig was. They probably didn't use the word back in Boston, but he didn't know what else to call the festivities the men probably planned. It sure as heck wasn't a soiree, or whatever word a lady might use. It didn't matter. He couldn't leave Faith here, even if the men were planning a tea party.

He snapped the reins and turned the wagon around. "I'll take you to my home, Faith. I know that's not going to be to your liking, but you can't stay here by yourself."

He half-expected her to throw herself off the wagon, or at least demand that he stop and let her off. Instead, she stared at him with a look of complete horror.

"I know it's not proper."

"It's not proper," she whispered.

"Now, Faith, don't make me put you under house arrest." He smiled at her, hoping his comment might make her give him an answering smile.

Instead, she looked even more panic-stricken.

"This isn't Boston," he said, his tone stern. "If I don't take you to my home, I'd risk your safety and well-being. I promise to behave honorably."

They rode in silence. His conscience troubled him greatly, but what could he do? There was no place for her. Even the hotel in Magnolia wouldn't do on account of all the rough cowboys that came through town. He wished he could say something to reassure her that she'd be safe with him.

After a while, she spoke. "Is your son there?"

"Yes, Caleb's there. He lives with me. I don't know what Grace wrote about me and my brothers, but I can promise you that none of us would ever hurt a woman."

He braced himself for outrage or distress. He was certain that his insistence on taking her to his home would be the end of any chance he had with her. If she wasn't making firm plans to return to Boston now, she would when she stepped inside the home he shared with Caleb and Lucas. He groaned at the thought of bringing such a refined lady into the house.

There was none of that, however. Instead, she sat with a resolute expression on her face. She wasn't merely resigned. Stoic was more like it.

"I like Texas all right," she said.

"You do?"

"Would you..." Her words trailed off.

"Would I what?"

Soft laughter spilled from her lips. His heart leapt at the sweet sound.

"Would you let me steer the mule team?"

"The – what?"

"Let me take the reins. For just a short while."

He scoffed. "I've never ridden in a wagon driven by a woman."

She lifted her chin. "Neither have I."

Her sass peeked past her wariness, and he had to admit he liked that side of her. Shaking his head, he handed her the reins. She wrapped her fingers around the leather and glanced at him for some reassurance. He nodded, but with a rush of reckless impulse, wrapped his hands around hers.

"Hold them a little tighter, Faith. You gotta show the mules that you're in charge."

He enveloped her hands with his and felt warmth spread across his palms. To his surprise, she didn't pull away, but allowed him to hold her hands for a short spell. He drew them back. He couldn't hold her hands all the way home, despite how much he might want to.

"Thank you," she murmured, her eyes sparkling with happiness. "I've never even seen a mule, much less driven a mule team."

"This is a terrible idea," he grumbled good-naturedly.

"Lately," she said with a soft laugh, "terrible ideas are the only kind I have."

He wasn't certain if she included him in that category, but he found himself laughing along with her. He wasn't entirely happy about her driving the wagon, but the team plodded along, unconcerned. And the expression on her face was all he needed to convince him to give in. As much as he gave Matt a bad time for wanting to turn himself inside out for Grace, Thomas could see the appeal.

"Am I one of your bad ideas, Faith?"

She didn't reply right away. Thomas wasn't certain if she'd grown reticent once again, or simply thoughtful. After a moment she spoke. "Exchanging letters with you was Grace's idea. Not mine."

"True," he said. "I've got to admit, you're a bit of a surprise. Grace told me you're mighty reserved. I never imagined I'd meet you when you stepped off the train with a bag of stolen Spanish gold."

"And I never imagined I'd come face to face with you while sitting in a Texas sheriff's office."

Thomas couldn't help feeling pleased. Faith's pretty smile had returned, and that made him happy. It might not last. In fact, he was certain it wouldn't. Her smile would definitely fade when she met Lucas. Or when she faced a plate of scorched scrambled eggs for the third time.

Chapter Eleven

Faith

Faith clung to the hope that Thomas was as good a father as he'd led her to believe in his letters. Surely a man who loved his son wouldn't mistreat a woman. That was what she told herself.

She'd watched him intently, noting how he'd treated everyone from his prisoner, Bing, to the mule team. While Thomas was a tall, clearly powerful man, he had a gentle nature. To her surprise, she felt almost at ease around him. His boy, Caleb, had a similar kind demeanor. They looked nothing alike, but both spoke in a thoughtful way that made her fears fade ever so slightly.

The brother, Lucas, on the other hand, was an entirely different matter.

Caleb and Lucas met them at the door of the house. Lucas had Thomas's eyes, and pleasant looks, but was dark-haired and seemed to have an aversion to a razor. His short but scruffy beard made him look like a swashbuckling pirate from one of Hope's books. He seemed bemused by her arrival.

The boy just stared, slack jawed.

After Thomas introduced them, he told Caleb to tend to the mules. The livery man would come for the animals soon, but in the meantime, they needed feed and water.

Caleb seemed not to hear a word and continued to gape at her.

"Son," Thomas said gently.

When the boy didn't reply, Lucas smacked him across the top of his head. Faith didn't care for his rough treatment. Not one bit. She was surprised at the slow burn of resentment that came over her. She imagined reaching over and smacking Lucas, to give him a taste of his own medicine. She'd never entertained anything so outrageous before, but today was a day of first times.

The poor boy looked raggedy and unkempt. His hair stuck up at odd angles. His sleeves were several inches too short, exposing his thin arms. She yearned to mend the worn elbows of his shirt, or better yet, sew him a new one entirely.

Caleb shook his head as if trying to gather his scattered thoughts. "If Faith's here, I got stuff to do."

"You need to mind your father," Thomas said, lifting her valise from the back of the wagon. "Do that first and then you can go about your business."

The boy frowned. "Yes, sir."

He jumped down from the porch, not bothering with the steps, and led the mule team to the barn.

Faith followed Thomas into the house, trying to tamp down her alarm. He took her to what appeared to be a sitting room. It was a far cry from Mrs. Caldicott's sitting room. It contained an odd assortment of furnishings, mostly wooden chairs with broken wicker backings. A couch sat under a window, piled high with boxes of dusty books. The shelves were empty.

"I'll be right back," Thomas said. "I need to talk to my brother about dinner."

Faith nodded. When he left, she went to the window to look out at the surroundings. The barnyard looked tidy and well cared for, she noted. It was in far better order than the interior of the house. Somewhere in another part of the house, Lucas and Thomas argued about what to make for dinner.

She waited for Thomas to return, feeling an overwhelming awkwardness. The door slammed, footsteps echoed in the hallway and Caleb appeared in the door.

He grinned at her, his arm behind his back. "I brought you something."

"You did?"

"Yup, a present."

"How lovely," she replied hesitantly. "You shouldn't have."

"But I wanted to, Miss..."

"Call me Faith, please."

He beamed at her. "Close your eyes."

"Er... all right."

She heard him take a few steps toward her.

"Now open them," he said.

She did as she was told, opening her eyes to find him standing before her with a small, bedraggled bunch of flowers in his hand.

"Ladies like flowers, right?"

"Why, Caleb, what a kind gesture. I'm afraid I don't care for flowers. They often make me sneeze. It's the pollen. Cats make me sneeze too."

He looked incredulous. "Cats?"

She nodded.

"What about dogs?"

"I don't believe they do."

He hurried to the front door. She moved to the window, wondering what he might do next. The flowers sailed past the window, landing on the ground outside. A moment later, he was back.

"My dad said I should show you to your room. Said it might be more fitting if I did than if he did."

"Thank you."

He picked up her valise and motioned for her to follow him upstairs.

"I didn't know when you were coming, but I made sure when you did, you'd have a nice room. I even borrowed a pretty bed cover from Aunt Grace."

Her heart leapt at his mention of her sister. "How is my sister? I'd hoped to see her, but the little one is sick. They're not at home."

"Aunt Grace is wonderful."

Faith let out a sigh. His words were a comfort to her. She would have far preferred to see that Grace was doing well with her own eyes, but she trusted the boy's assessment.

He trudged along the hallway, carrying her bag with some effort. She wanted to ask if he could manage, but before she could, he pushed open the door of a bedroom. He set the bag down in the middle of the room and held out his arms.

"What do you think?"

The room was a sunny, pleasant room, with a chest of drawers in the corner, and a bed on the opposite side. A colorful quilt covered the bed. The room was cheery enough, but the bed sagged in the middle. Faith moved closer and studied the alarming droop in the middle of the bed.

"Want to sit down, give it a try?"

She tried not to grimace. It wouldn't do to be a bad guest her first night with the Bentley family. She lowered to the bed, testing the mattress. The bedding gave way and she fell back, sinking into a deep crevasse. She yelped and flailed, trying to escape the abyss. Caleb hurried over, grasped her hand and pulled her free.

"I worried about that one," he said.

Faith straightened her dress and ran her hands over her hair. A pin had come free while she tussled with the ancient bedding. She peered into the depths, wondering if she might find her hair pin. Caleb spotted it before she did, reached in and retrieved it. Without a word, he yanked the quilt off the top of the sagging mattress, picked up her bag and, dragging the quilt on the floor behind him, left the room.

"I can show you another bed. Might be a little better."

She followed him to the next room. He gestured to the bed. She edged toward the bed and patted the top with a tentative hand. Lowering slowly to the bed, she expected to encounter another soft and worn-out mattress. This time the bedding had as much give as plank of wood.

"I don't mean to be so much trouble, Caleb, but it's not very comfortable."

He nodded. "I was afraid of that. There's another bedroom. It's in the attic. You'd be off by yourself. I'd hate for you to get lonesome."

"Lead the way, Caleb," she said, hoping she sounded cheerful. "Maybe this bed will be just right, baby bear."

He stopped to look at her, a hurt expression in his eyes. "Ma'am, I'm eleven. I'm not a baby."

"I'm sorry, Caleb. I was making a joke, or trying to. You know the story of Goldilocks?"

He blinked and to her dismay, she saw that his eyes watered. "No, ma'am."

She drew closer and brushed his hair from his forehead. "No one ever read Goldilocks and the Three Bears to you?"

He turned away and moved down the corridor, heading to the narrow staircase at the end. "Never heard of it."

Faith stared at his retreating figure. Her eyes prickled. A lump formed in her throat.

"You coming, Faith?"

"I am indeed." She hurried after him.

The room at the top of the stairs was furnished in a similar fashion as the other rooms. Just a bed and dresser but filled with sunshine. She peered around the corner and found a small alcove, a sort of turret with a majestic view of the fields and horizon.

Caleb came to her side. "Pretty up here, isn't it?"

"My goodness, it is. I've never seen such a view. Life in a city doesn't offer much in the way of pretty vistas. I could just look at this forever."

"Forever?"

Something in the boy's voice drew her from her reverie. He regarded her with a solemn expression. The lock of hair had fallen over his forehead again and she wanted to brush it away. It seemed that he didn't welcome her touch, however. He'd almost flinched when she'd tried to brush his hair away before. There was a note of longing in his voice that made her heart ache.

She wanted to comfort him but didn't want to suggest that she really meant forever.

"What I meant to say is that the view is lovely. I could look at it for a long time."

He pressed his lips together. "Right. Do you think the bed is okay?"

She hadn't tested the third bed because she'd been so taken with the lovely scene outside her windows. The rolling fields bathed in soft evening sunlight riveted her attention. "I'm sure it will do. For now."

Chapter Twelve

Thomas

He had to admire the girl's determination. She'd sat through a dinner of burned eggs, and listened to Lucas go on about calving season. She even pretended to be interested in Caleb's stories about teaching Buster his latest trick. Either she was trying hard, or she was a good liar.

It didn't bother him if she was lying to him, but if she was misleading his son, he'd have plenty to say about that. The boy had voluntarily bathed and come to the table dressed in clean clothes. To her credit, Faith hadn't noticed his dirty clothes earlier, but she probably couldn't know how hard the boy was trying to make a good impression.

Faith had asked about her sister's welfare several times over dinner. In return, Lucas had given her a bit of a bad time.

"You think she spends every day wishing she could escape our evil clutches, don't you?" He gave her a teasing smile.

She took a dainty bite of her food, chewed it and swallowed. "I'm responsible for Grace coming to Texas."

"You are?" Caleb asked.

"I was ill last winter with pneumonia. The doctor said I should move to a warmer climate. When Grace heard that, she made the decision to make the trip first."

The kitchen grew silent.

"I owe her a debt," Faith said quietly. "I'd never forgive myself if..."

Her words faded. She blushed as she looked around.

Caleb nodded. "You'd never forgive yourself if Aunt Gracie had been trying to escape the evil clutches of Uncle Matt?"

Faith smiled. "Something like that."

"Good luck breaking her free," Lucas said. "Matt is mighty sweet on his wife, and she on him. You'll see. And when you do, you might send a note to your younger sister that we're not a bunch of wild heathens here in Texas. We're plenty refined."

Thomas held back a grin. Lucas made no secret of the resentment he held towards Hope.

"How did you like your dinner?" Lucas growled.

Faith folded her hands and gave him a prim look. "Delicious. Thank you for cooking. I'd like to tidy the kitchen, if you don't mind," she added.

Lucas gave an indifferent shrug.

Thomas added a few more points to her score. She certainly held her own against Lucas, who seemed eager to challenge their house guest. Caleb shot him an anxious look as if he fretted that Lucas might ruin his chances for keeping Faith around.

Lucas grunted a few words that didn't sound like appreciation but weren't flat-out insulting either. He and Caleb excused themselves, both heading to the pen to check on a new calf.

"I'll help you with the dishes, Faith," Thomas said. "You've had a long day."

He set a kettle on the stove and brought a bucket of water from the pump. He wanted to tell her that John's house had a pump at the sink. If they were to marry, she'd live in a fine home. He didn't want to press his luck. He knew she was taking in the lay of the land and wouldn't make any decisions until she determined that Grace was well.

She gathered the plates and took them to the sink. "I think I insulted Caleb today."

"What makes you think that?"

"I made a thoughtless comment. I feel terrible."

"He seems fine."

She gave him a grateful smile and began washing the plates. He stood beside her, took the soapy plates and rinsed them in the bucket. He was distinctly aware of her small, feminine form next to his. She seemed so utterly fragile and out of place here in his rough and cluttered home. Earlier that day she'd been almost afraid of him. Now she spoke easily as they shared a quiet moment.

"How do you like Texas so far?" he asked, echoing the question he'd asked earlier.

"I'm not sure. I almost got arrested on my first day." Her lips tugged upward, and her eyes sparkled. "But then I got a chance to drive a team of mules, which was exhilarating. And it made me think..."

Her words trailed off. Her face turned pale as she stared past his shoulder. He followed her gaze to the pie safe on the other side of the kitchen. A large rat perched on top.

"It's some sort of rodent," she whispered.

"I think it's one of Caleb's pets," Thomas said. "Don't worry."

She gripped the counter, swaying unsteadily on her feet. "His pet?"

"Right."

A small cry spilled from her mouth. "It j-just ran away. Where is it now?"

"He didn't go far. Don't worry."

"Kindly stop saying that." She darted to the table and clambered atop a chair. "I hate rats. And mice."

The rat emerged from below the pie safe. Thomas picked it up even though he didn't care for rats either. He shrugged and went out the back door to the shed behind the house. He set the rat inside one of the cages that lined the wall. When he returned to the kitchen, he found Faith still on the chair, regarding him with a mixture of fear and disbelief.

"Sometime Herbert gets out of his cage. He likes to come inside."

"Herbert?" she whispered. "The rat's name is Herbert?"

"I think so." Thomas scratched his head. "Maybe. Unless..."

"Unless what?"

Her voice sounded shrill, a hair's breadth from a full panic.

"Unless that was Henrietta."

She opened her mouth as if to reply, but nothing came out. After a moment, she snapped it shut. He wasn't sure what he thought about her standing on the chair. He was starting to feel a little sorry for her and the last thing she needed today was to tumble off the chair onto the hard, wooden planks of the kitchen floor.

Crossing the kitchen, he held out his hands in a conciliatory gesture. A let's-be-reasonable posture. "Let me help you down."

"I'm not getting down, Thomas. Not until Grace returns. Then I'll get down long enough to run out of the house as fast as I can."

He bit back a chuckle, sensing that she wouldn't see the humor in the situation.

"I understand you're worried. How about I carry you to your room? It's getting late. I'm sure you'd like to settle in for the evening."

She recoiled. “You can’t carry me. I’m up on the third floor. I’m too heavy for you.”

“Come on now. You’re just a little speck of a thing. Let me help you upstairs.”

“How do you know there aren’t any rats upstairs?”

“They come to the kitchen because of the food. They want Caleb to feed them some treats.”

She narrowed her eyes.

He clasped her hand, drawing nearer. When she didn’t flinch or pull away, he smiled at her. “Besides, rats are afraid of heights. They won’t go upstairs.”

Scooping her into his arms, he half-expected her to shriek, but she didn’t. He strolled out of the kitchen and started upstairs. She looped her arms around his neck and let out a small murmur of dismay as they ascended.

“You feel as light as a feather,” he murmured.

“I don’t believe you.”

He grinned as he turned down the hallway to the staircase that led to the third floor. “I think Texas is growing on you. Just think. You met Herbert – or Henrietta, not sure. And you didn’t even start with your hiccupping.”

Her eyes widened. She looked like she might agree with him, but out of pure stubbornness, refused. Going up the second, narrower staircase proved to be a little more difficult, but he managed to get to the top, only bumping his head twice on the overhang.

“Here you go, Miss O’Brian,” he said gallantly, setting her down. “Would you like me to check under the bed?”

She smoothed her hands down her skirt. “What for?”

“In case Caleb’s pet garter snake got loose.”

She scoffed, edging away from him. “Nobody, not even Caleb, would have a pet snake, for heaven’s sake.”

As much as he was tempted to argue, he let it go. Caleb liked all sorts of critters. The shed out back was a veritable Noah's Ark, but he knew he'd better keep that small detail to himself. She might start with that hiccupping yet.

Chapter Thirteen

Faith

Faith woke the next morning just as the sun crested the horizon. She dressed hurriedly and went downstairs to find Caleb and Thomas already up. They met her at the foot of the stairs, both smiling at her as she came down the steps.

"Good news," Caleb said. "Your sister's back in Magnolia."

"Oh, my word," she whispered, hardly daring to believe her ears.

"I can take you over as soon as I have the wagon hitched," Thomas said. "I know you're keen to see Grace."

Faith was so very eager, that the moment the wagon was ready, she let Thomas help her up. As they made their way down the lane, she realized they'd left before she'd had a bite to eat or packed her belongings. She chided herself. She hadn't even taken the time to don a bonnet. She'd arrive at Grace's home looking a sight, but she didn't care. All she wanted was to find her sister doing well and happy.

They didn't have far to go. Still, the trip seemed to take an age. It had been almost six months since she'd seen Grace. All that time apart, she'd worried and fretted, imagining the worst. When she closed her eyes at night, she often pictured Grace living a life in Texas that was filled with misery.

She shuddered at the thought.

"Hey, now. What's troubling you?" Thomas asked.

"I'm just so anxious to finally see her. That's all."

When they arrived, Grace stepped out of the front door and hurried down the steps. Faith didn't wait for Thomas to help her down. She simply clambered down to the ground once he'd set the brake and rushed to embrace her sister.

"Grace," she said softly. "I've missed you so."

"And I've missed you." Grace drew back and gazed into her eyes. "Every minute of every day."

Grace linked her arm through hers and led her up the stairs to a bench on the porch.

"When I heard you were here in Magnolia, I could scarcely believe it," Grace exclaimed. "I'm almost too astonished for words."

Faith feasted her eyes on the sight of Grace. Her sister blushed and ran her hand over her stomach, showing off the gentle curve. Faith drew a sharp breath and ran her fingers across Grace's waist.

"Is that my little niece or nephew?" Faith whispered.

"Yes, it is."

A man emerged from the house. He wore a friendly smile and could be none other than Matt. He looked very much like Thomas, save for the scars on his face. When Grace first got to Texas, she wrote to explain that her husband had been attacked by a wild animal as a young boy. The scars weren't ghastly, but Faith knew Matt felt ashamed of the old wounds.

"Why, hello, Miss O'Brian. Fancy seeing you here," Matt said.

"You can just nod, if you would rather not speak to him," Grace said. "He knows you're reserved."

"It's all right," Faith murmured. In a stronger voice, she greeted her brother-in-law. "Hello, Mr. Bentley. I'm pleased to meet you."

Faith noted the puzzled look Matt gave Grace.

"My confidence has grown somewhat since I've come to Texas," Faith said.

Caleb and Thomas came up the steps. Thomas grinned at her, mischievously. "She's had a number of adventures since arriving to Magnolia."

"Adventures?" Grace and Matt asked in unison.

"What kind of adventures?" Caleb asked.

The boy stared at her with an incredulous expression, as if he doubted she were capable of any sort of adventure. To her chagrin, Grace and Matt wore the same disbelieving expressions. Thomas, however, smiled at her as if the two of them shared a secret. She realized with growing dismay, that they did, indeed, share a secret. Not that she wanted to withhold anything from her sister, but now was not the time to divulge her brush with a criminal element.

Or being questioned in the sheriff's office.

Or the rat in the kitchen.

Faith patted Caleb's shoulder. "I'll tell you about my adventures, Caleb. All in good time."

Grace arched her brow.

"It's nothing to worry about. Besides, I want to hear all about your new life here with your growing family. Where's Abigail?"

"Sleeping, thank goodness. She was up half the night with croup."

Faith drew a sharp breath.

Grace gave her a tired smile. "She gave us a scare, but she's doing better. I've spent the night rocking her and praying."

"My word," Faith whispered.

Grace took her arm and led her off the porch. They walked past the gardens that surrounded the house through a gate and out to a sunny terrace overlooking green pastures. A table had been set with a sumptuous breakfast. The aroma of freshly baked bread wafted on the morning breeze. Platters of bacon and fruit and sausages greeted her eye. Her stomach rumbled.

Grace squeezed her arm. “I heard that.”

“I am quite hungry,” Faith confessed. “I haven’t had a decent meal since I left Boston.”

“What’s that?” Grace asked. “You don’t care for Lucas’s cooking?”

Faith shook her head. “Poor Caleb. Poor Thomas.”

“I invite them to eat with us, but they’re too proud. The Bentley men are impossible.”

Faith looked over her shoulder and caught Thomas’s eye. A warmth crept over. “Yes, they are quite impossible.”

He returned her teasing words with a wry grin. It seemed they shared a secret communication. With just a glance, she knew what he was thinking, and he seemed to understand the same. How had that happened? She’d been terribly afraid to stay in his home. Yet something had changed in the short time in his home. She’d faced her fear, and when she confronted her near-constant dread, it had slunk away, defeated.

She was almost sorry that she’d be leaving Thomas’s home. She’d miss him and Caleb.

Matt and Thomas wandered to the edge of the terrace. Caleb followed behind, his gait and posture matching that of his father and uncle. Faith took a chair across from Grace, hardly able to tear her eyes from the boy.

“Something about Caleb, trying so hard to be a man, steals my breath,” Faith said.

“He’s a dear boy. He’s been practically counting the days till you arrived. I should scold you for not writing more, or at least to tell us that you were coming.”

Grace poured each of them a cup of tea. The fragrance of the freshly brewed Earl Gray reminded Faith of having tea in Mrs. Caldicott's sitting room, thousands of miles away. Despite the fond memory, her thoughts drifted to Grace's comment about Caleb. It puzzled her.

"He wanted to write you," Grace said.

"Caleb?"

"Yes, Caleb." Grace's tone held a subtle note of reproach.

"Whatever for?"

"Thomas told me he wanted to know if he could call you 'mamma'." Grace's eyes misted. "He's never had anyone to call 'mamma'."

Faith bit her lip and studied the boy as he spoke with the men. Thomas nodded in agreement with something Caleb said and tousled his hair. The boy's mop of hair looked as unruly as ever and Thomas's affectionate gesture didn't help matters.

"I didn't realize," Faith murmured. "How could I have known? I assumed he would resent a woman coming into his home."

She cringed as she recalled the tiny bouquet of flowers he'd picked for her.

"I'll try to do better, although I'm not sure if I'm up for the role of mother. I hardly know if Thomas and I are compatible."

"You seem compatible enough. I saw the looks you two exchanged. I knew it all along."

Faith frowned at her sister. It wasn't like Grace to be so forceful. Faith could see that Texas had changed her sister too.

"I'll be certain to visit him and spend time with him," Faith said. "Perhaps I can make up for my thoughtlessness."

Grace drew a deep breath. "I'm sorry, Faith, but the doctor gave us strict orders. We're not to have anyone in our home until Abigail is well."

Faith recoiled. "What? But I could help you, so that you could get your rest."

Grace shook her head. "He was adamant."

"Do you mean to tell me that I'll need to remain with Thomas?"

"I know it's awkward, and perhaps a little unseemly."

Faith stared at her sister, hardly able to comprehend her words. "A *little* unseemly?"

Grace gazed at her, with a look that radiated pure happiness. "I can hardly believe you're here. Now we just need to put together a plan to entice Hope to come to Texas."

"But..." Faith hardly knew what to say. "You're abandoning me with those men?"

Grace set her cup down and leveled a stern look at her. "It's partly your fault. You should have written to tell us you were coming. Now you'll simply have to make do. Just for a little while. I suggest you go into town to pick up provisions from the mercantile."

"Provisions?"

Grace's lips quirked. "Unless you prefer Lucas Bentley's fine cooking."

Chapter Fourteen

Thomas

Caleb was, of course, elated that Faith returned with them, not just to collect her belongings, but to stay until Abigail recovered. For the next few days, he did his best to show off the ranch. He fretted that their home wasn't fancy enough for her and yearned to take her to John's home. The old farmstead was properly furnished and, in general, tidier.

Which wasn't saying much.

It had been months since John died, and a year and a half since his wife passed. The old homestead was probably musty and in desperate need of a woman's touch.

"I've shown Miss Faith everything there is to see here," Caleb grumbled over breakfast. "She's been here three days and it's probably getting a little boring."

"I'm not bored," Faith said, helping herself to more scrambled eggs.

"Look at that," Lucas said. "Faith's having seconds!"

Thomas could tell his brother was impressed that Faith not only didn't complain about the food but seemed to enjoy it. She never failed to compliment him and thank him for cooking.

"But I would like to go into town in the next day or so. Grace gave me a list of provisions that the mercantile should have on hand. And I have a letter for my sister, Hope."

Lucas scowled at his eggs. Ever since Hope had told him she didn't think she wanted to come to Texas, he'd been growling like a lion with a thorn in his paw. He shook his head but didn't say anything to Faith. Thomas thought that in the last few days, Lucas had demonstrated a grudging but growing respect for her.

"Maybe I ought to ride along," Lucas said. "Just in case the Grimes brothers are looking for Faith."

Caleb paled. "What?"

Faith smiled across the table. "I haven't told you about my adventure, have I? If you like, I'll tell you all about it when I tell you your next bedtime story."

Caleb's ears turned red with embarrassment.

"Bedtime story?" Lucas scoffed.

Thomas felt both a rush of warmth for Faith and sympathy for his son. Lucas enjoyed tormenting the boy and would tease him endlessly over this. Lucas had no patience for Caleb's boyish yearnings, often telling him to act like a man.

He was about to tell Lucas to leave Caleb be, but Faith spoke first.

"Now, Lucas, don't be unkind," Faith chided. "Last night, I told him about Goldilocks and the Three Bears. Every child should know that story."

"If you say so," Lucas said, his mouth curving into a wicked grin, one that suggested he had no intention of abiding by her words. He added a high-pitched, "Mamma Bear."

Faith narrowed her eyes at Lucas. "And if you embarrass Caleb in front of the cowboys, you'll have me to contend with."

The kitchen grew quiet as the Bentleys all stared at Faith. Thomas couldn't imagine what she meant by that, but noted the fire in her eyes, as did Lucas and Caleb, no doubt. For a long moment nobody replied, until finally Lucas relented.

“Yes, ma’am,” Lucas replied, his tone bordering on meek.

Caleb snickered at his uncle’s lapse of bad manners, and Thomas was certain he saw Faith’s lips tug upward.

Thomas had chores that needed doing, but he didn’t want to spend time apart from Faith. Over the past few days, he’d come to look forward to seeing her in his home or wandering the property with Caleb by her side. Any day Faith and Matt might come calling to say that the baby was well, and Faith could stay with them, and then she’d be gone. The notion left him with an empty feeling.

He managed to convince Lucas to do his chores. He then hitched the wagon and made good on his offer to take Faith and Caleb to the Bentley homestead. It was a fine, autumn day, with deep blue, cloudless skies. A cool breeze blew, giving a hint of the cold weather to come.

Thomas relished sitting next to Faith. Caleb rode in the back along with his dog. Buster was a nuisance, but Caleb promised the dog was getting better every day and would behave.

When they arrived at the homestead, Thomas was struck by how desolate the house appeared. Faith seemed to notice as well. Her expression grew solemn as they drew near. He stopped the wagon and set the brake.

Thomas brushed the cobwebs from the doorway and pushed open the door. The hinges squeaked, protesting months of disuse. Inside, white sheets lay draped over the furniture. Thomas set his hand on the small of Faith’s back, ushering her past the front foyer.

“This is the parlor,” he said. “I have a lot of happy memories of this room. My brothers and I spent every evening here after dinner and after our chores were done.”

Faith walked around the room, taking in the details. “You boys were happy?”

“Very happy. We squabbled like all brothers, but mostly we had fun together. Mamma would make us read every evening, a half hour of the Bible, and a half hour of whatever we wanted. Then we were free to do as we pleased. Sometimes we’d play a game. Other times we pushed the furniture back and wrestled until Daddy came storming in.”

Faith bit her lip. “Did he get very angry with you boys?”

“Sure, he’d start off raising heck, but then pretty soon he’d start wrestling too. He’d chase us around, pretending to be a mean old giant. Pretty soon, Mamma would be in here, fussing at all of us. Especially if she heard something break, like a chair. Couple of times it might have been a window.”

Faith looked stunned at his words.

“Well, it was bound to happen,” Thomas said sheepishly. “We got pretty wild.”

Outside, Caleb played with Buster, throwing a stick for him. His laughter rang in the air, but the house was quiet.

“It’s kinda spooky in here, isn’t it?” he asked, wandering around the room. “I half expect to hear my mother call me for dinner.”

She crossed the room and stopped before the fireplace. His gaze traveled down the narrow expanse of her shoulders to her slender waist. Returning to the house was bittersweet, but he liked seeing Faith in front of the fireplace. The memory of cold winter nights spent around a roaring blaze made his heart squeeze.

“Houses don’t like to be empty, do they?” she said quietly.

“You could marry me, and we could have a passel of children.”

She turned abruptly. Her lips parted with surprise as she searched his face.

"Thomas," she said quietly. "I didn't know you wanted more children."

"That makes two of us."

She swallowed hard and turned away. Lifting to her tiptoes, she reached for a ceramic vase that had belonged to John's wife.

"Want me to get that for you?" he asked.

The vase tipped over the edge of the mantle. Faith cried out. The vase tumbled down and with a deafening crash, it hit the wood floor.

Thomas rushed to her side, crushing the shards beneath his boots. "Are you all right, Sweetheart?"

She looked up at him, her face a mask of terror. He clasped her hands in his, searching for any sign of injury, then he tugged her away from the broken pottery. Urging her to a chair, he yanked the cover aside and coaxed her to sit down.

Her feet, clad in dainty leather shoes, looked to be unharmed. She wasn't injured, thank goodness, but she was visibly shaken. The color had drained from her face and she began to tremble violently.

"Sorry," she breathed. "I'm so sorry."

Tears spilled down her cheeks.

"Faith, don't cry," he whispered. "You're breaking my heart."

"I didn't mean to m-make a mess."

"It's just a vase. Nobody cares." He glanced over his shoulder and saw that there was a matching vase at the other end of the mantle. "There's another one. Want me to go break it?"

Without waiting for an answer, he got to his feet, strode to the fireplace and smashed the vase on the floor. He turned, giving what he hoped was a winning smile. “See?”

He moved slowly, crossing the room, hoping to comfort her somehow.

She whimpered and held up her hands. “I’m so sorry.” Her eyelids fluttered. She swayed unsteadily, sinking in the chair. Thomas lunged to her side as she collapsed in his arms.

Chapter Fifteen

Faith

Faith had little recollection of the trip back to the Bentley home. She woke the next morning, fully dressed, lying in her bed. Someone, Thomas she assumed, had taken off her shoes and tucked her into bed, clothes and all. Shame burned inside her. She could hardly stand the idea of coming face to face with him after yesterday's debacle. She'd acted like a fool. And he'd taunted her for her outburst, by smashing the other vase.

The memory frightened her beyond reason. The sound of the vase shattering rang in her ears. She'd been reminded of the times her father had shouted and broken things, terrorizing her mother and sisters.

Thomas Bentley was a beast. Worse than a beast. And while she lay incapacitated, he'd tucked her into bed. It was an outrage.

She didn't have long to wait. She found him standing at the bottom of the stairs, his arms folded over his chest.

"You're looking a little better," he said matter-of-factly.

"I'm feeling fine, thank you."

"I thought I'd ask if you wanted to go to town, to mail your letter and whatnot."

While she didn't want to spend any more time with Thomas, at least not today, she had to admit she needed to go to town. Grace had sent a few small gift baskets over the last few days with jams and jellies, but she still needed to buy proper ingredients for meals. "That would be agreeable. I'd also like to stop at the mercantile to buy a few things."

"Like what?"

"Provisions."

"Provisions? What sort?"

"Anything but eggs."

Lucas poked his head out of the kitchen. "Getting tired of eggs, your highness?"

She gave him a haughty look, hoping that would put an end to his teasing. Had Thomas told his brother about her ridiculous behavior? How utterly mortifying. Lucas shrugged and retreated to the kitchen.

"It seems Grace has abandoned me here with you... men. I suppose I might as well procure a few necessities."

"All right," Thomas said, a smile curving his lips. "I'll take you in myself. That will give us a chance to have a little chat."

The smirk on his face exasperated her. He seemed to think the whole thing was some sort of joke. She wished she could go into town with anyone else, but the only other person who could take her was Lucas. She didn't relish the idea of spending time with him either. She gritted her teeth. This was Grace's fault. She was certain of that and would tell her so at her first opportunity.

A short while later, they were on their way to Magnolia. Thomas tried to wring the truth out of her over the rumbling of the wagon wheels.

"What was that all about?" he demanded. "Last night. All that carrying on."

"I don't wish to discuss it."

"I deserve to know why you were so afraid yesterday." He jerked his thumb to his chest. "Of me. Why is that, Faith?"

She pressed her lips together, feeling somewhat like an obstinate child. If she were feeling a little more sure of herself, of *him*, she might share some of her past. But his demanding tone upset her. She didn't want to discuss anything with him when he spoke to her in such a domineering manner.

They rode the rest of the way to town in silence.

When she'd come to Magnolia a few days before, she hadn't paid much attention to the town. Now, she took the time to study the small shops and busy streets. Cowboys rode through the streets, and twice, Thomas had to stop the wagon to allow the cowboys to move a herd of cattle past.

The dust made her cough. Thomas took a handkerchief from his pocket and offered it to her. "Cover your nose and mouth."

"Thank you, Thomas."

The cattle ambled past in what seemed like an endless stream of animals, magnificent in their sheer number. If she were feeling stronger, she would delight to see the cowboys at work. Thomas and Lucas owned cattle and Caleb had told her about their cattle drives. After the herd passed, Thomas drove the wagon to the livery and helped her down. To her surprise, he offered his arm. She took it with a small murmur of surprise. He was gallant even though he was clearly irritated with her refusal to answer his questions.

First, they went to the post office. Faith bought stamps and mailed her letter to Hope. The next stop was the mercantile, a bustling, crowded shop filled with stacks of crates and sacks of grain and flour. Thomas led her to the back where she gave her order to the shopkeeper.

Thomas eyed the list with surprise. "Ten pounds of flour?"

"For bread. Unless you prefer the leftover bread from Mrs. Patchwell."

"Five pounds of sugar and two sides of bacon?"

"Is it too much?" she asked with dismay. "I made a list from Grace's recommendations."

"It's not too much, if you don't mind doing all that baking and cooking for us."

She gave him a small smile. "I want to do this for you and Lucas. And especially Caleb."

Her heart lightened a little and perhaps Thomas felt the same way, judging from the way his eyes lit with a gentle look. Amidst the bustle of the shop, they shared a glance that felt like a truce of sorts.

"I'm sorry if I frightened you," he said softly so that only she could hear. "If you tell me what I did wrong-"

She touched his arm lightly with her fingertips. She wanted to confide in him. One day. Not today, and certainly not here. As she struggled to find the words, she heard a man call out over the din of the mercantile.

"Why, hello, Thomas."

Faith peered into the crowd, searching for the person who spoke. A man pushed his way through the people. He was nicely dressed, clean shaven and wore a pair of spectacles. It took a moment for her to realize it was the same man who had been incarcerated in the jail the day she'd arrived in Magnolia.

"Hullo, Bing," Thomas said. "You remember Miss O'Brian."

Bing's smile faltered. "*Miss*? I thought you'd decided to marry."

Faith felt people's eyes on her. Her face warmed with embarrassment and without realizing, she stepped closer to Thomas. She was grateful when he clasped a protective hand around her elbow.

"I'm mighty hopeful Miss O'Brian will do me the honor," Thomas said. "You're looking well. Keeping out of trouble, I assume."

A few people standing nearby chuckled, including Bing.

"Yes, sir, turning over a new leaf, you might say. I've got a new client, a very important new client, you might say. A wealthy man, a Mr. Montgomery. He and his wife are interested in adopting a young man here in Magnolia."

By now, the bystanders had resumed their shopping. No one paid attention, but Faith noted an immediate change in Thomas. His eyes flashed with fury.

Bing stepped closer and lowered his voice. "I told him you were married."

"That's none of his concern, or yours for that matter."

Bing sighed, looking solemn. "I need to speak to you immediately."

Chapter Sixteen

Thomas

Thomas read the sign on the law office door. *Theodore Giddings – Attorney.* He wondered how Bing went from Theodore to Bing but didn't bother to ask. He had more pressing business.

Bing opened the door and motioned for Faith and him to enter. Thomas ushered Faith inside, noting the bewildered look on her face. He couldn't help feeling a little dazed as well. Bing's words had shaken him to his core. Maybe Bing wanted to get even for the nights he'd spent locked in the Magnolia jail.

Hopefully.

Bing sat down behind his desk. "Have a seat."

"I don't think so," Thomas said.

Bing shrugged. "Mr. Montgomery wants to adopt Caleb."

Faith sank into a nearby chair, giving a small gasp of dismay.

"Over my dead body," Thomas said.

"Montgomery says Lorena was in the family way when she married you."

Thomas curled his hands into fists. He glanced at Faith before responding. She was pale, stricken looking, and stared at him with shock.

"It's true," Thomas said.

"And am I to believe you were responsible?" Bing asked.

Thomas turned away, moving to the window as he mulled his options. Everyone knew Caleb was born five months after he and Lorena married. But few people, aside from his brothers, knew that he and Lorena had never been together as man and wife. He certainly hadn't touched her before the wedding. Even after, they'd lived apart.

He hadn't wanted to have marital relations with a woman who carried another man's child. For years, he'd hidden the truth of his marriage. Never did he imagine his painful past would return. He pictured Caleb. His heart squeezed with pain, imagining how the boy would react if he knew any of the sordid details surrounding his mother.

He couldn't lie to Bing and claim the boy. It wasn't in him. And if he claimed he'd fathered the boy, Faith would likely run from his home as fast as her feet could carry her.

"I don't see how that's any of your business, Bing."

Bing chuckled. "Well, it's not. You're right. Montgomery says he can offer the boy more than you can. He says the boy is getting to the age where he should go off to school. He's thinking of some military academy in Mississippi. But more importantly, he's married. When he told me that he felt the boy needed a proper family, I told him you'd married too."

Thomas turned to face Bing. "You what?"

Bing raised his hands in a conciliatory gesture. "I was trying to tell him he didn't have grounds to sue you for custody of the boy. Normally I wouldn't discuss a client's wishes with you, but this is different. You've always treated me decently. I know you're a good father. I was trying to help matters. When I told him you were married, he seemed to back off."

"But I'm not married."

"That presents a bit of a fly in the ointment."

"Is that your legal opinion?" Thomas snapped.

"More or less," Bing said. "If I were you, I'd be mighty concerned that Mr. Montgomery might pay a visit to his grandson. He's entitled to see the boy, you know. And try to tidy up the place a little. Get Caleb a haircut and tell him to take a bath every so often. Land sakes, let's hope Montgomery doesn't meet Lucas."

Thomas grimaced.

Bing went on. "If he does come to the ranch, make sure you take him to visit Matt and Grace."

"Why?"

Bing tilted his head toward Faith. "So he can meet Miss O'Brian, of course."

Thomas scowled. Faith wasn't living at Grace's home, of course, but he didn't feel inclined to share that with Bing. Faith lifted a trembling hand to her lips.

Bing went on. "Course, the best solution is to get married as soon as possible. Montgomery isn't going to take no for an answer. I told him I likely wouldn't take the case and now he's talking to fat cat lawyers in Houston."

Thomas scrubbed his hand down his face. Fury welled up inside him. What if the man came to the Bentley ranch today, or tomorrow? What if he was out there now? He closed his eyes and said a quick prayer the man wouldn't come pay a visit.

"Come on, Faith. Let's go."

Faith rose immediately, went to the door and waited for him, wide-eyed and pale.

"I'm not happy about any of this, Bing, but I do appreciate you telling me," Thomas said.

"Yes, sir," Bing said. He gave Faith a polite smile. "Miss O'Brian, it's a pleasure seeing you again."

"Thank you," she replied quietly.

By the time they'd made their way back to the livery, the wagon had been loaded with the provisions. Thomas didn't bother to return to the shop. The shopkeeper would tally the bill and put it on the Bentley account. He helped Faith onto the wagon and turned for the ranch.

Chapter Seventeen

Faith

Faith tried hard to avoid thinking of what the lawyer had told them. The notion that relative strangers could pluck Caleb from his home was beyond comprehension. The look on Thomas's face had hurt her heart. Was it shame?

Instead of dwelling on the Old Man Montgomery she tried to brighten Thomas's mood over the next few days by cooking her best recipes. She'd imagined cooking for the Bentley menfolk ever since her first meal of scrambled eggs. She hadn't wanted to offend Lucas though. What was more, she hadn't been entirely certain how long she'd remain with them. She'd hoped to be staying with Grace by this time.

But Grace had all but abandoned her.

Faith was certain. The reason she was certain was because Caleb had returned from Matt and Grace's home that afternoon with tales of showing off Buster's tricks for Grace and Matt. And Abigail, too.

"Buster sure made Abby laugh," Caleb said, munching on an oatmeal cookie Faith had just taken out of the oven.

Muttering under her breath, she imagined giving her sister a piece of her mind. Abigail sounded as if she'd recovered, yet Grace hadn't sent for her, or even inquired about her well-being. It was just as well, she supposed. Thomas needed her here, and she intended to help him as much as she could. She finished peeling the potatoes for dinner and sliced them. The cookies cooled on the counter. Caleb reached for another one.

"Mind you don't spoil your appetite before dinner," Faith said gently.

"Miss Patchwell says I have a hollow leg, that it's impossible to fill me up."

"Wait till you see what I'm making for your supper."

"It smells real good."

"*Really* good, Caleb."

"Yes, ma'am."

"I'm making a dish my mother used to make us, called Dublin Coddle."

The boy's eyes widened. "Sounds odd. Never heard of it."

She opened the oven, and with dish towel in each hand, carefully eased the Dutch oven out. She set the heavy cast iron pot on the stove. When she removed the lid, a burst of steam rose, filling the kitchen with a savory aroma. Sausage and streaky bacon sizzled amidst the chopped onion. She put a layer of potato slices over the top of the meat, arranging them so they covered the dish.

She could feel Caleb's attention on her as she worked. "This is what we're having for dinner." Lowering her voice, she whispered. "No eggs tonight."

"It looks real good," Caleb marveled. "I mean really good. I've never seen anything like that in my life."

She put the lid back on and set the dish in the oven to cook for several more hours.

"Just you wait. And if you mind your Ps and Qs I'll make another batch of cookies tomorrow."

"More cookies?" His tone was incredulous.

"More cookies. Jam thumbprints, but only if you agree to my terms."

"What do you mean?"

She lifted a pair of scissors and snapped them in the air. "You need a haircut, Caleb Bentley."

Caleb looked aghast. For the next ten minutes he tried his best to convince her that his hair was 'jus' fine' and he didn't mind if it got in his eyes every so often. When Faith raised the threat of no more cookies, he relented. They went to the front porch. There she sat him down on a chair and proceeded to trim his hair.

Faith took her time, hoping she would do a good enough job. She'd trimmed her sisters' hair before, but never the hair of a fidgety boy. He wriggled plenty, but at least he allowed her touch, something he'd been hesitant to do when she first came.

He chattered on about the family of mice he'd found in the barn and how he wanted to put them in the shed but had decided against it on account of her living with them, and her dislike of rats and mice. Faith couldn't help but smile at his stories.

"I sure do like having you here," he said.

His words caught her unawares. She set her hand on his shoulder, giving him a gentle squeeze.

He set his hand on hers. "I've never been happier. You make our place feel so special."

She swallowed, trying to dislodge the lump in her throat. "I've never been happier either," she whispered.

He smiled, patted her hand and let his hand fall to his lap. "Even if you make me get a haircut," he grumbled.

The late afternoon gave way to dusk. Soon Lucas and Thomas returned to the house. Thomas looked very much as if the weight of the world rested on his shoulders, but he managed a tired smile when he saw her finishing with Caleb's haircut.

His eyes met hers and held her gaze as he ascended the steps. "Faith, thank you."

Caleb left the porch, mumbled his gratitude and darted inside, probably to pinch another cookie. Lucas followed a step behind. Faith could hear them squabbling over the cookies in the kitchen.

"Sure is nice to come home and smell dinner cooking."

"I hope you like it."

"And you're making Caleb look a little more presentable. How'd you get him to sit still long enough for a haircut?"

"With a promise of cookies."

"I hadn't ever tried that."

She patted the chair in front of her. "The shop is open if you'd like a haircut."

With a soft laugh, she marveled at her own audacity. Why, she was practically flirting with Thomas! She hardly recognized herself.

He ambled closer, stopping a half pace away from her. He stood so near, it stole her breath. His scent overwhelmed her thoughts. He smelled of leather and hard work and an outdoorsy scent that was all his own. She gazed into his warm eyes as he took off his hat and combed his fingers through his hair.

"You think I need a trim, Miss O'Brian?"

She blushed at his sultry tone and felt tingles race across her skin. Swallowing hard, she asked the question that had tormented her since the day they'd gone to town. "Do you think Bing is right? Will Mr. Montgomery try to take Caleb?"

He shrugged. "Probably. He's not one to make idle threats. He never did care much for me. I'm sorta surprised he's waited so long. Something set him off."

"Like what?"

"Don't know. He's an older fellow. He and his wife only had Lorena and they had her late in life. Maybe he's facing his own mortality without any other kin around."

This was the first time he'd said her name aloud. A jolt of envy hit hard, scattering her thoughts like dry leaves on an autumn wind. She should be worried about Mr. Montgomery, trying to help Thomas with this terrible possibility that loomed over all of them. Instead, she thought about his late wife. Lorena... She tried to envision Caleb's mother and pictured her as a breath-taking beauty.

"You loved her...?" She said the words, softly whispering the question she hadn't meant to ask. "I'm sorry. I have no business asking you that."

"I didn't," he said quietly.

He didn't love her. A wave of relief fell over her, and she hated herself for that. She felt small-minded. Her thoughts swung from envy to distress. Pain squeezed her heart as she imagined Thomas in a loveless marriage. She lifted her hand and tentatively reached for him. When he didn't pull back, she cupped his jaw and stroked the rough barb of his beard.

In the days since she'd arrived at the Bentley home, he'd kept his distance from her. Not now. Covering her hand with his, he spoke in a gentle tone. "This doesn't scare you?"

She shook her head. "No. A little, maybe."

"Are you planning on fainting?" he asked, with a hint of a teasing smile curving his lips.

"Thomas..." she said quietly. "Can we forget that happened?"

“Only if you tell me why it happened.”

She wanted to pull her hand back, but he held her, keeping her near with the gentle press of his rough hand.

“I thought you’d be angry with me. That you might lose your temper.”

“Like your father lost his temper?”

She shuddered at his words. “Who told you?”

“Gracie told me and Matt both. But it doesn’t matter. What matters is that I’ll never lose my temper with you or threaten you in any way. Never.” With that, he turned her hand and pressed a kiss to her palm.

Chapter Eighteen

Thomas

He was awake. Again. Even though he'd been up before dawn, in the saddle by daybreak, and worked all day out on the range searching for lost calf and mother pairs, he wasn't tired enough to sleep, apparently. Lying in bed, he tried to picture Faith sleeping in her bed upstairs.

It had been three days since Bing had warned them about Caleb's grandparents. In that time, little had changed. He was beginning to wonder if Bing had been straight with him.

Grace and Matt had visited, coming without the baby, and swearing up and down that Abigail needed just a few more days without visitors. He smiled as he recalled the way Faith had given her sister a pointed look. Later, when he saw Matt and Grace off, Grace had winked at him.

He wasn't entirely sure if he felt gratitude or frustration. Naturally, he loved having Faith in his home. But each day, each *hour*, he grew more attached to her as did Caleb. He'd considered offering for her, but thanks to Bing, any offer he made would be freighted with implications. If he asked and she said yes, it might be out of a sense of obligation. If he asked and she said no, it might be because she wanted no part of a bad situation.

Lorena had married him under duress, after she found herself in trouble. He certainly didn't care for the idea of Faith marrying him unless it was what she wanted with all her heart.

He growled, threw back the blankets and stalked across the room. Light from the full moon cast his bedroom in a silvery light. Opening the door, he remained motionless, listening, for what, he didn't know.

Clad in nothing more than a pair of pajama trousers, he was hardly decent. Despite his state of undress, he moved down the hallway, stealthy and light on his feet, trying to keep the floorboards from squeaking.

First, he went to Caleb's room. He pushed the door open. Moonlight filled the boy's room and spilled across his bed. Beneath the silvery light, Caleb slept peacefully, his long, coltish limbs sprawled across his bed.

Thomas felt both a fullness and an emptiness like he'd never felt before. He recalled the nights when Caleb was just a baby and he'd come to his room to check on him while he slept in his crib. It seemed like yesterday. He loved the boy more than he ever imagined he could love anyone, or anything. And now, the thought that someone might take him away, filled him with despair beyond words.

It could not be possible for Mr. Montgomery to take his boy. He'd fight it any way that he could. Shutting the door, he turned to look up the stairwell to the room where Faith slept. It was an outrageous scandal that she remained in his home without being married to him. It was hardly an example to young Caleb, and yet, she fit in their lives so perfectly he couldn't fathom being parted from her.

With a weary sigh, he returned to his room and got dressed. Sunrise was an hour off. He could use the time to work on the ranch accounts. He went downstairs, lit the lamp on his desk and sorted through his papers. Lucas had gone to the post office the day before and brought back a stack of mail. Thomas opened the first letter on the stack, a note from a ranch owner in South Texas, seeking information about the Bentley's Brahma bulls. He set it aside for Lucas, who ran the relatively new venture.

Footsteps drew his attention from his work. Faith appeared in the doorway, dressed for the day, but with her hair loose and falling past her shoulders. The way she carried herself, with the prim posture of a schoolmarm, contrasted with the lovely disarray of her unbound locks. Her bright eyes held a spark of humor and her lips tilted upwards with the hint of a smile. He wondered what her lips would feel like if he kissed her.

"Good morning," she said.

He realized he was staring like a fool, but couldn't stop himself. "Your hair is longer than I realized."

She smiled demurely. "I meant to put it up, but I saw your light and wanted to ask if you'd like coffee."

"And it's sort of wavy at the ends."

"Especially when it's damp," she said with a bemused tone.

"You always smell nice." He waved his hand, searching for the right words. "Like flowery things."

"I'm glad you think so." She laughed softly. "Coffee?"

He nodded. Her skirts swished as she turned for the kitchen. A few moments later, he smelled the aroma of fresh coffee. Usually, it was Lucas who made coffee in the morning. There was something about having Faith nearby that changed everything about their home. Her feminine presence brightened his world, a world he hadn't even realized was lacking.

Distracted by thoughts of her, he opened the next envelope, a letter from a judge in San Antonio. He'd assumed the missive would be about ranch business. To his surprise, the judge summoned him to his court to discuss 'the welfare and keeping of Caleb Thomas Bentley.'

"What is it?" Faith asked.

He looked up to find her standing in the door, holding a steaming mug.

"Is it bad news?" She set the coffee on his desk.

"You might say that." He handed her the letter.

After she read it, she set it down beside his mug. "Did you notice?"

"Notice what?"

"The letter is addressed to Mr. and Mrs. Thomas Bentley."

Chapter Nineteen

Faith

Thomas and Faith arrived in San Antonio, dusty, tired and with no time to spare before the appointed time. She'd fretted about the fact that the judge presumed that she and Thomas were married. She also wondered why Caleb wasn't going to be present at the meeting with the judge.

"It's better this way," Thomas said as he led her along the walkway toward the judge's offices. "I don't want to upset the boy unnecessarily."

"What will you tell the judge about our marriage?"

Thomas stopped to face her. "I'll tell him that Bing misunderstood."

She winced at the implication of his words. "Would it help if you told him we're engaged?"

He grinned at her. "I'm certain it wouldn't hurt our case. He'll take one look at you and know right off that I'd be one lucky man."

She blushed. "Thomas."

"I haven't even asked you."

"You don't need to. I accept. Besides, there's no time."

"I wanted to propose. You know that, don't you?"

"Please. Stop teasing me."

He tucked her hand under his arm and they ascended the steps to the courtroom. "I'm not even close to teasing you. I promise to ask you properly. Go down on one knee, say something nice about your pretty eyes."

"Hush, Thomas. Be serious."

"I am serious."

He opened the door for her and set his hand on her lower back as they entered. The gesture gave her a rush of pleasure. A young man sat at a desk in the foyer. He greeted them and asked them their business. Thomas showed him the letter and the man ushered them to the judge's chambers.

Faith had expected to be admitted to the courtroom and was very thankful that wasn't the case. Somehow, a smaller, less official space intimidated her less. She breathed a sigh of relief as they walked down the corridor.

Another couple sat in the waiting area, an older gentleman and his wife. The woman curled her lip when she saw them, and the gentlemen scowled. Faith felt Thomas tense and it dawned on her this was Mr. and Mrs. Montgomery, Lorena's parents. The picture of Caleb's happy, grinning face came to her mind. Not in a thousand years could she imagine these people, these dour and unpleasant people, raising Caleb.

She turned away with a shudder as she and Thomas entered the wood-paneled chambers. The judge sat at his desk. He looked up from his work and motioned them in.

"Mr. and Mrs. Bentley, I'm Judge Murdoch." He gestured to the chairs. "Please take a seat. I wanted to speak to you before I discuss my decision with the Montgomerys."

"Thank you, sir," Thomas said, his tone resolute. "Before we get started, I'd like to point out that Faith and I are engaged to be married. We are not married presently."

Judge Murdoch folded his hands and peered at them over his spectacles. "I see."

Faith sat beside Thomas. She held her breath, wondering how the judge would view Thomas's words. Given the way he furrowed his brow, it seemed that he was displeased. Her heart thudded heavily. This man, a perfect stranger, had the power to decide Caleb's fate.

"Mr. and Mrs. Montgomery argue that Caleb isn't your child. Is that correct?"

Faith turned to look at Thomas. His jaw was set with grim determination, and in an instant, she knew the answer to the question. Caleb wasn't his. She'd suspected as much when Bing had first broached the subject. And now that horrible man and woman wanted to use that to get Caleb in their clutches.

Thomas's expression darkened. "I don't see what-"

"Answer the question, Mr. Bentley."

Faith's heart ached for Thomas, and Caleb too.

"What difference does it make?" she blurted. When the judge narrowed his eyes at her, she added a hasty, "Your Honor."

Thomas gave her a look of surprise. She, herself, felt surprised. It wasn't like her to challenge an authority figure. She shrank back in her chair. Clenching her jaw, she prayed she wouldn't start hiccupping, like a fool.

"Well, Miss... I'm sorry what's your last name?" the judge asked.

"O'Brian, sir."

"I like to see children situated with their own flesh and blood."

Faith knew he awaited her reply, but despite her trepidation, she couldn't bring herself to nod or agree. She remained quiet, refusing to concur with his words. From the corner of her eye, she noted Thomas's somewhat surprised expression. This territory was familiar to him. He was a sheriff and used to all sorts of people. She was a lady's companion. She'd made her way in the world by being agreeable, not by arguing.

"Are you fond of the boy?" the judge asked. "How eager are you to raise up another woman's child?"

"Very eager," Faith said quietly. "I'm very fond of the boy, and I believe he feels the same about me."

"You wouldn't pose as Mr. Bentley's fiancée just to help him, now would you, Miss O'Brian?"

Dismay stole over her, making her thoughts spin wildly. She hadn't imagined that the judge would question her, or not on this point. It was her own fault for speaking up.

"No, sir."

Dear lord, would lightning strike her down, right here in a judge's office?

"Have you set a wedding date, Miss O'Brian?"

"Well, you see, the problem is that I can't get m-married just yet."

He winked at her. "Cold feet?"

"I don't have cold feet, sir!" In her growing panic, she turned to Thomas, hoping he'd offer some sort of help.

He gave her a blank look.

The idea came to her in a flash. "I don't have a wedding dress. I intend to use my sister's, but it will require me to make some alterations."

She gave a breathless laugh, one that was followed by a hiccup.

The judge frowned. "A glass of water, dear?"

She shook her head.

"I'm in a bit of a predicament, you see. I believe that Mr. Bentley is an excellent parent to Caleb despite the fact he didn't father the child. I'm aware of the good sheriff's excellent reputation. In fact, I have already written my response to the Montgomerys. However, my favorable decision was solely because I understood Mr. Bentley to be married."

"Oh," Faith her voice weak. "Drat."

The judge nodded. "Drat indeed."

"I can think of a solution to my predicament. I can simply marry the two of you."

"Marry us..." Faith whispered.

Judge Murdoch rubbed his hands together, a delighted smile curving his mouth. "Excellent."

Chapter Twenty

Thomas

When they left the judge's chambers, the Montgomerys were still sitting in the waiting area. Thomas avoided their glare, focusing his efforts on guiding Faith out of the office. She kept her gaze straight ahead and clasped his arm with an iron grip.

An hour before dark, they were back in Magnolia. Instead of taking her to the home he shared with his brother, he took her to the homestead. He took her hand and led her up the steps into John's home. They hadn't spoken much on the way home. Not that he didn't have plenty to say, but he wanted to bring her to the Bentley homestead when he spoke the words.

She looked around the foyer first and then searched his eyes for the meaning of their stop at John's home.

"I never intended for you and me to get married in that way," he said, holding her hands. "I wanted you to marry me willingly."

"I did, Thomas. If that's what you want, it's what I want too." She gave him a timid smile. "I was just a little taken aback. I hadn't expected that and would have liked to have had Caleb and Lucas there, along with Grace and Matt, of course."

"I would have liked that too." He wanted to pull her into his arms and kiss her. When they'd said their vows, he'd pressed a quick kiss to her cheek. At the time, he hadn't been sure if she'd welcome even that small gesture.

"I've been very happy since I've come to Magnolia," she said. "Happy to be with you."

"I want to keep on making you happy, sweetheart. I'd like to live here, in a proper home." He felt as awkward as a school boy, but he pressed on. "I would like to share a life with you, and God willing..."

He hardly dared say the words aloud.

"Go on," she said gently.

"I'd like to have children. More children."

He felt like someone had hit him with an iron anvil. Why was Faith so calm?

"I'd like children too. One day, after we've had some time to know each other a little better."

He nodded. She wanted to wait, of course. He could hardly blame her, and yet he felt a small pang of disappointment. He yearned for her touch more than he could say.

She squeezed his hands. "Show me the house. I promise not to break anything."

He chuckled and set about to show her the home he'd grown up in. It was spacious, and, aside from a little dust, far tidier than the home they shared with Lucas. Upstairs were three bedrooms and a nursery. The washroom didn't have running water, but he told her that would be easily remedied. They walked hand-in-hand through the rooms and returned downstairs.

"How soon can we move in?" Her voice was tinged with excitement. Her eyes sparked with happiness.

"Tomorrow." He ran the back of his hand over her jaw and gazed into her eyes. It pleased him beyond measure that she liked the home and was eager to move in. Living here with her and Caleb seemed like a dream that was about to become true.

Hoofbeats interrupted the tender moment. They went outside to find Lucas loping up the drive. He pulled his horse up in front of the house, a thunderous look on his face. Lather covered his horse's neck and the animal's nostrils flared. For some reason, Lucas had seen fit to gallop all the way to the homestead.

"What's got you all riled up?" Thomas demanded.

"We had company today," Lucas snarled. "The Montgomerys sent one of their men to talk to Caleb."

"The hell you say?"

"I sent him on his way, believe me. We brawled right there in the barnyard. Caleb came running to see what all the cussin' and hollerin' was about."

Thomas felt a burn of rage. "That's some nerve. The judge decided in our favor."

"I figured he would. Unfortunately, the son of a gun told Caleb."

Thomas felt his mouth go dry. His throat tightened. "What did he tell Caleb?"

Lucas shook his head and grimaced. "Everything."

Thomas thought he might explode with fury. What kind of man would tell a kid his father wasn't who he thought it was? He curled his fists, wishing he could have been there to confront the man himself.

He forced himself to regain control. Now was not the time to allow his heated emotions to take over. His son needed him. Thomas would just talk to Caleb, man to man. Caleb wasn't a man, yet, of course, but he deserved the truth. Thomas would lay it out for him. What happened was in the past. The circumstances of Caleb's birth meant nothing to Thomas. He needed to explain that to the boy and make him believe that.

Faith came to his side and set her hand on his shoulder. "Let's go talk to him."

Chapter Twenty-One

Faith

If the drama surrounding Caleb had one unexpected outcome, it was that Grace and Matt came to visit that evening. They hurried over the moment they heard that the Montgomerys had sent someone to collect the boy. Miss Patchwell came with them, holding the baby, Abigail.

Thomas invited Matt to his study to talk over the turn of events. The two men disappeared behind closed doors and were joined a few minutes later by Lucas. Faith prayed the three Bentley brothers would arrive at a way to get past this entire catastrophe.

Meanwhile she turned her attention to the other visitors. Faith had heard about Mrs. Patchwell but hadn't met her yet, thanks to Grace practically banishing her from their house. The woman was as kindly as Faith had imagined.

"So lovely to finally meet you, my dear," she said, giving her a broad smile and clasping her hands. "We're so pleased you've come to Texas. I hope the Bentley men have been treating you well."

"Very well, thank you."

Mrs. Patchwell's face grew solemn. "Poor Caleb. Where is the dear boy?"

"Upstairs, in his room," Faith said. "He's refusing to come out."

"I'm sure his heart is broken." Grace held Abigail on her hip. She shook her head and grimaced. "What a terrible thing to have happened. Blood isn't the only thing that bonds people. I feel every bit as devoted to Abigail as I do to the baby I'm carrying."

"Of course, you do, Mrs. Bentley," Mrs. Patchwell murmured. "I'll just run upstairs and speak to Caleb myself, if that's all right with you, Miss O'Brian."

"If you think that will help," Faith said.

Grace smiled. "Mrs. Patchwell and Caleb are devoted to each other."

Mrs. Patchwell went up the stairs. Faith heard her knock on the door and a moment later the door opened.

"Would you like to sit on the porch?" Faith asked. "Maybe little Abigail would let me hold her."

They went outside and sat side-by-side on the bench. Faith held out her hands to the small girl, but Abigail drew back, nestling deeper in Grace's arms.

"She's going through a shy spell right now," Grace said apologetically.

"She's darling. It's so sweet to see the two of you together."

Grace kissed the top of the child's head. She gave Faith a contrite look. "Have you forgiven me for leaving you here with the Bentley menfolk?"

"It hasn't been all bad." Faith gave her a coy look.

"Really?" Grace's eyes sparked with mischief. "Are you and Thomas getting along? Is there hope?"

"You might say there's hope."

"Tell me," Grace demanded.

"I should keep you in suspense in return for abandoning me with two bachelor men and a young boy. I can hardly believe you would stoop to such ploys."

"Go on. Tell me if you and Thomas have taken a liking to each other."

"You might say that."

Grace gasped. "Tell me more."

Faith went on to tell her sister about the events in the judge's office and how she and Thomas had exchanged their vows that very morning. Grace stared at her in disbelief.

"What could I do?" Faith asked. "If I didn't agree, he would have awarded custody of the boy to the Montgomerys."

"Astonishing. And here I'd imagined that you'd wear my dress and we'd have a wedding. I'm not sure if I'm delighted or disappointed."

Faith bit her lip. "Right now, I'm too fretful about Caleb to think of anything else. Thomas and I visited the Bentley homestead this afternoon. We spoke about living there, the three of us. I think Thomas wants to offer me more of a home. Although, I'm perfectly happy here."

Grace nodded and gave her a tired smile. "I'm so pleased to hear that. I can't tell you how much. I just wish the circumstances were different."

"As do I," Faith said quietly.

The front door opened. Mrs. Patchwell came out with Caleb beside her. The boy kept his eyes downcast, but Faith could see that he'd been crying. Her heart ached. How she wished she could take his pain away from him and suffer in his place. Regret welled inside her. If she'd married Thomas right away, the Montgomerys might not have tried to take Caleb.

Mrs. Patchwell set her hand on the boy's shoulder. "Caleb says he'd like to know his grandparents."

Faith cringed inwardly. Of course, he'd want to know his kin. It made perfect sense, and yet she could only imagine how Thomas would take the news.

Caleb sniffled and wiped tears from his face.

"Do you want your father to take you?" Faith asked.

The boy flinched when Faith said the word "father". He shook his head.

Mrs. Patchwell patted his shoulder and gave Faith a sympathetic look. "He'd like Lucas to take him for a visit."

Caleb ran back into the house without a word. Faith heard him race upstairs and slam his door.

Mrs. Patchwell sighed. "Maybe it's for the best that Thomas let him go for a spell."

When Faith didn't respond, the woman said a few words about letting the two sisters talk privately and went back inside.

"Dear Lord," Faith whispered. "What if Caleb wants to live with them?"

Grace shook her head. "Don't let yourself think of the worst."

"The reason Thomas asked me to come to Texas was to be a mother to Caleb. What if..."

Faith couldn't finish. She fell against the back of the bench, sinking under a wave of despair.

Chapter Twenty-Two

Thomas

Caleb wanted to know his grandparents and who was he to deny the boy his wish?

Lorena's parents left Magnolia after she passed away, swearing they wanted nothing to do with the town, Thomas or Caleb. Old man Montgomery bought a small ranch and raised sheep. The notion of raising sheep didn't set well with most cattle ranchers and Thomas was no exception. He'd wanted to tell Caleb about the sheep but resisted. Let the boy find out on his own.

The night before he was to leave, Thomas lay in bed, tossing and turning. He couldn't sleep, thinking about Caleb leaving in the morning. He got out of bed and wandered down the hallway to Caleb's room, but the door was closed. He set his palm on the door and fought the pain in his heart.

Throughout the evening, he prayed, asking for the strength to let Caleb go. Since he'd returned from San Antonio, the boy had hardly spoken to him. In a way, it seemed that Caleb was already gone. Thomas rested his forehead against the door and waited for the ache in his heart to fade, but it only deepened.

Turning away, he scrubbed his hand down his face. He went to the stairs and glanced up at Faith's door. It was closed too. They were married now, and he would have liked holding her in his arms. Resting near her would ease his pain, but now wasn't the time for any of that. The time would come, though, and that notion was the only thing that lightened his burden.

He returned to his room, telling himself that everything would turn out fine. Caleb would meet the Montgomerys, get to know them a bit, and return to the Bentley Ranch where he belonged. But when dawn broke, and it came time for Caleb and Lucas to set out, Thomas could barely bring himself to say goodbye and watch them ride away. Faith stood with him, silent but resolute.

"It's just a few days," she said quietly.

"The Montgomerys don't even know they're on their way," Thomas said, his voice choked. "Caleb didn't want me to write to them. I think he's worried they might have changed their mind about him."

"The poor boy."

"He worried about you changing your mind too."

Faith frowned. "When?"

"Before you got here."

She drew a sharp breath. The mood over the last few days had been somber. Neither Thomas nor Faith mentioned the fact that they'd exchanged vows which meant that Caleb and Lucas didn't yet know.

"Caleb just wants a home and a family so bad," Thomas said.

Faith tried to coax her lips into a smile. "That's what I want too. What about you?"

He pulled her into his arms and held her for a long moment before speaking. "You know I do."

"Then let's clear the dust from the homestead. By the time he returns, we'll have it ready."

For a moment, Thomas felt too surprised to respond. He waited for her to say more. His lips curved into a reluctant smile. He shook his head. "You're willing to do that?"

She narrowed her eyes, pretending to look perturbed with him. "I'm not willing to tidy the homestead. I demand the chance to clean and tend to the house. It's been empty too long. And besides, you promised me."

Chapter Twenty-Three

Faith

Later that morning, they walked through the homestead door. Faith couldn't help feeling a glimmer of hope. Maybe, with a little luck and a lot of prayer, they could turn the forgotten house into a home.

First, they opened the windows to air the rooms. A cool autumn breeze moved through the house, dispelling the musty smells. Next, they took an inventory of the furnishings and linens and rugs. Faith had to smile at Thomas, her big strapping husband. He counted the bed sheets, one by one, sorting through the delicate sheets with his work-roughened hands.

"I like working with you," she said, jotting down the number of pillowcases he had stacked.

"It's a good thing too," he replied. "With the two of us being old marrieds and such."

Throughout the morning, he'd been stoic, but now he almost allowed himself to smile. She laughed softly at the notion of being an old married couple. And yet, the prospect of growing older with this man sent a rush of happiness through her. She wished things were different, of course, but she loved working with him, shoulder to shoulder, setting up the house that they would share.

Sometime around midday, Miss Patchwell arrived with a basket and a cast iron pot filled with chicken and dumplings.

"It smells wonderful," Faith marveled, setting it on the iron stove. "I've heard all about your cooking."

"From whom?" Mrs. Patchwell demanded good-naturedly.

"My sister."

"Ah yes, well, she's a wonderful cook." Mrs. Patchwell sniffed. "I'll give her that."

Faith smiled. She'd heard how much Mrs. Patchwell relished her position as cook. When Grace arrived, it seemed the woman had fretted about losing her job since Grace's cooking was so well received. From what Grace had written since then, Faith was certain of how much Grace and Matt esteemed Mrs. Patchwell. Faith was certain that the woman's job was secure. Especially since her sister had a little one on the way.

"It was so kind of you to bring a meal," Faith said.

"It's the least I can do. How is Thomas holding up?"

Faith glanced out the window to see Thomas working by the barn. He was knocking down old wasp nests and spider webs with a broom. All day, he'd toiled tirelessly.

"I think he's determined to make a home here for Caleb. Something a little better than what he had growing up. He said he never noticed what a difference having a woman in the house made."

Mrs. Patchwell smiled. "From what I hear, it's a wife he has now. The rascal. Marrying you without so much as a proper wedding, cake and flowers, and whatnot. We're all feeling a little cheated."

Faith blushed but gave her an answering smile. "It was spur of the moment."

"When Caleb returns with Lucas, we'll have a fine party for the two of you."

Faith's heart ached at the thought of Caleb returning. She prayed that he wouldn't somehow be swayed by the Montgomerys to remain with them. She drew a trembling breath.

"Don't you worry yourself, dear," Mrs. Patchwell said. "That boy will be back. Mark my words."

Faith's eyes stung with tears. She nodded.

"I'd best be going," Mrs. Patchwell said.

Faith saw her off, waving as she disappeared around the bend in the path. The late afternoon sunshine warmed her as she stood on the porch. A few minutes after Mrs. Patchwell left, Thomas came to the house, a weary smile on his face.

"I wondered if you might like to spend the night in your new home, Mrs. Bentley?"

She drew a sharp breath. It was the first time she'd heard him say her married name. She smiled as a pleasant warmth spread across her skin. Her sleeves were rolled up. She rubbed the goosebumps on her bare arms and shivered.

He grinned, took her hand in his and rubbed her arm. "You like the sound of that as much as I do?"

"I do."

"Well? Would you like to spend the night here? You can take the big bedroom at the end of the hall, and I'll take the one by the washroom?"

She nodded. He glanced down at her arm, and when she followed his gaze, she realized his attention was on the scar she'd gotten as a girl. Her first impulse was to yank her arm back, but she resisted, despite her shame.

"What happened here?"

"My father... he dropped a plate and the shards cut me."

Thomas arched his brow and gave her a skeptical look.

"He threw it." She swallowed hard. "At me."

Thomas grimaced, lifted her hand and kissed the scar.

She was touched by his tender gesture and allowed him to fold her into his arms.

"He wasn't well after his injury. He always regretted his fits of rage," she whispered.

"I'm sure he did," Thomas murmured.

He stroked her shoulder and kissed the top of her head. She closed her eyes and rested her cheek against his broad chest. She felt both protected and cherished. His masculine scent made her want to linger in his embrace.

"Today, I was supposed to comfort you," she whispered. "Not the other way around."

"You have been a comfort to me. Thank you for coming here with me. If I didn't have your company today, I'd be hurting even worse."

She sighed with contentment. Despite the sadness of the day, she felt a small glimmer of hope. The house was lovely. She could imagine the three of them living happily in the old homestead. Not that she objected to the other house, but it was clear that Lucas felt it belonged to him.

"I won't let anyone hurt you, Faith," he said quietly. "I'm your husband now. Your protector. I'm all yours for better or for worse, and I have been from the first moment."

She looked up at him. "I'm glad."

He lifted her chin and lowered to brush a kiss across her lips. A soft murmur of surprise welled in her throat, but she didn't protest his attention. Instead, she let him press another, deeper kiss, one that made her tremble. He'd kissed her when they exchanged vows, but not since then. This kiss was entirely different than the chaste kiss he'd given her before.

His lips were soft, a stark contrast to the bristle of his jaw. He let his hands drift down to her waist and skimmed the curve as he tugged her closer. Her thoughts spun as she lost herself in his arms.

"Thomas," she whispered.

"What?" he asked, a teasing lilt to his voice.

"You can't kiss me like this when Caleb returns."

"Why not?"

She could hardly keep from smiling at him. "What sort of example is that?"

He scooped her into his arms. She let out a gasp of surprise and looped her arms around his neck as he carried her inside.

Thomas frowned and shook his head. "We're doing this in the wrong order, darlin'. I should have carried my bride over the threshold first thing, not after we've been here all day."

He put her down in the kitchen and kissed her once more. "Can't hardly feel miserable when I can steal kisses from a pretty girl," he said. His expression sobered. He lifted her hand to his lips and kissed her. "Thank you, Faith."

Chapter Twenty-Four

Thomas

Their first night in the homestead, Faith told him that she'd never kissed anyone before. Since then, he'd managed to steal a few more. He pondered the notion of being her first kiss while he stacked firewood in the barrow. He couldn't help but feel a tad pleased. He'd never been a girl's first kiss before.

He yearned to kiss her last thing before he fell asleep and again first thing when he woke. When he'd hinted at his hope to live as man and wife, she'd blushed and fretted, saying a few words about waiting.

They'd lived in the house for three days now, and the sweet moments he spent with Faith shielded his heart from the pain of missing Caleb. Two days ago, they'd moved all their possessions into the house. They hadn't taken Caleb's belongings, however. Thomas couldn't bring himself to go into his son's room. He didn't want to see the boy's books, or boots or slingshot collection. It was too much to bear.

During the day, he fought the urge to saddle a horse and storm down to the Montgomery ranch. He wasn't entirely sure what he'd do when he got there, but the idea pleased him. Anything had to be better than just waiting. And waiting.

Faith emerged from the house to bring him a glass of lemonade. Her pretty face was lit with a sweet smile, one that never failed to thrill his heart. He brushed off his hands and met her halfway across the yard.

"Thank you," he said, accepting the drink. "It sure is mighty swell to have a wife."

Doubt made her features grow taut. "What if Caleb stays with the Montgomerys? You might regret having taken a wife."

Thomas frowned. "That won't happen, Faith."

"Which?"

"I can't say much about Caleb staying with the Montgomerys, but I know I won't regret marrying you. And I sure hope the feeling's mutual. Is that something I need to worry about?"

She laughed softly. "No."

He took a swallow of the lemonade. "Good. Because you're stuck with me."

Tapping her chin, she gave him a look that bordered on sass. "I suppose you're stuck with me, too."

He grinned. It seemed that his demure wife was flirting with him and he liked it very much. He set aside his drink, and clasped her waist, tugging her closer. "I don't know what I'd do without you here, Faith. I really don't. But I need to kiss that smart mouth."

She looped her arms around his neck. "If you must."

He lowered, claiming her lips with his. Her kiss tasted of sweetness and tenderness and devotion and all the things she brought to his home. She trailed her fingers across the back of his neck, threading them through his hair. Tightening his hold on her, he deepened the kiss, reveling in her scent and the feel of her in his arms.

It was a slow, lingering kiss, one that made his troubles fade from his thoughts.

"Faith," he whispered. "I love you. More than I can say."

She gazed up at him with surprise and a slow smile tilted her lips. "I love you too."

He lowered to kiss her again. The sound of a cough distracted him. He turned to find Lucas and Caleb, mounted on their horses, watching them. Caleb gaped. Lucas smirked.

"Sorry to interrupt," Lucas said, looking anything but sorry.

Thomas dropped his hands from Faith's waist but took her hand in his. "You've come back."

"Yes, indeed," Lucas said. "Mrs. Montgomery called Caleb incorrigible."

Thomas gritted his teeth but relaxed somewhat when he noticed that Caleb grinned.

Lucas set his hand over his heart. "Sort of made me proud, to tell the truth."

Thomas drew closer, still clasping Faith's hand. He could hardly believe his eyes. For days and nights too, he'd prayed for his son's return. He went to Caleb's horse and set his hand on the boy's knee, not sure what to say.

Caleb looked sheepish as he slid from the saddle. When he dismounted, he hugged Thomas, and then Faith. She had tears in her eyes as she wrapped her arms around him.

"Not time for a party just yet," Lucas remarked.

"What do you mean by that?" Thomas asked. Before Lucas could answer, Thomas heard an approaching wagon.

"Mr. and Mrs. Montgomery want to make sure you're not putting on a show of being married just to convince the judge. They've come to visit and see for themselves."

Chapter Twenty-Five

Faith

Between Mr. and Mrs. Montgomery, Faith wasn't sure who was more disagreeable. Both walked around the homestead, frowning, their lips pinched with clear disapproval.

"What time is supper served?" Mrs. Montgomery demanded.

Faith had shown the couple the downstairs, finishing the tour in the dining room.

"Whenever we're hungry," Caleb answered.

"I wasn't addressing you, young man," Mrs. Montgomery snapped.

Caleb leaned against the doorway with a sullen expression on his face. Standing beside him, Thomas gave the boy's shoulder a squeeze.

"Usually around six," Faith said. "Unless the men are riding in the pastures."

"Do you insist the boy eats his vegetables?"

"I haven't had to insist he eat anything. His appetite is prodigious."

"I beg to differ," Mrs. Montgomery said. "He hardly eats at all."

"I like Faith's cooking," Caleb said.

Faith drew a sharp breath.

He shrugged. "It's the truth."

Mrs. Montgomery waved a dismissive hand. “Such an ill-mannered boy, I’ve never met. Show me the upstairs.”

Faith looked to Thomas for help. The woman would likely want to know where everyone slept. Thomas winked at her and ushered the Montgomerys upstairs.

Thomas showed them the rooms and managed to avoid the question of where everyone slept, by explaining that he’d grown up in the house, and how many happy memories he and his brothers had.

“Do you intend to have more children?” Mr. Montgomery asked.

Thomas didn’t reply. Instead, he folded his arms across his chest and directed his gaze to Faith.

Faith felt her face warm as everyone looked at her. When a slight hiccup escaped her lips, she flushed even more. “Yes. God willing.”

Thomas lips curved into a smile. “I look forward to more children. The more the merrier.”

Faith said a quick prayer that her dratted hiccups wouldn’t return. When the Montgomerys announced they’d seen enough, she thought she might faint with relief. She and Thomas saw them out, and waved goodbye from the steps of their porch. Thomas looped his arm around her waist, tucking her against him as the couple left.

“Well, Mrs. Bentley, aren’t you full of surprises?” Thomas teased. “When do you suppose I might be able to have the pleasure of your company?”

“Hush, Thomas,” she muttered, her cheeks burning. “You’re incorrigible.”

Before he could draw her into another kiss, one that Caleb might witness, she slipped from his embrace. She excused herself with the comment that dinner wasn't going to cook itself.

She hurried to the kitchen to work on the evening meal. She prepared a meat pie, savory ingredients covered with a delicate pastry. While it baked, she set the dining table for the three Bentley men and herself. Stepping back from the table, she took in the sight of the way it looked set for four people. In the fading daylight, the table required a few candles. She lit them just as the men came inside and breathed a deep sigh of satisfaction.

Their first meal together in their new home.

Thomas said a prayer of thanksgiving. When he was done, he turned to Faith and smiled. "Everything looks wonderful."

They all agreed. Over dinner, Caleb chattered about the Montgomery's ranch and the fact that his grandfather was a sheep farmer. Disapproval edged his tone. He shook his head as he served himself another piece of the meat pie.

"Sure am glad to be home," he said, and dug into his food.

Thomas caught her eye. His eyes shone with emotion as he gazed at her. She didn't say a word but gave him a nod of complete understanding.

Neither Lucas nor Caleb asked much about Thomas and Faith's marriage. She found that fact somewhat amusing. Perhaps they both assumed it was a forgone conclusion. After apple pie for dessert, Lucas announced he and Caleb would head back to his house. He'd bring the boy back in the morning, along with all his belongings.

Faith wondered if Thomas might object, especially since he'd missed his son so very much. He didn't complain. He simply walked them out and said goodbye. Later that evening, after her kitchen was tidied, and the house was quiet, Thomas came to her room. He knocked softly on the door.

She sat on her bed, brushing her hair, clad in her nightgown. “Come in,” she said.

He pushed the door open, smiled at her and leaned against the door frame. “Looks like we’re stuck with each other.”

“It does look that way.” She sighed. “Stuck with each other… I never realized you were such a romantic.”

“I’m very romantic.”

She continued brushing her hair, trying not to smile at him. Instead, she schooled her features, giving him a skeptical look. “You’ll have to come up with prettier words than that if you want to convince me.”

His smile widened as he crossed the room, closing the distance between them. Gently, he took the brush from her hand and set it on her bedside table. He clasped her hands and drew her to her feet. The lamplight cast a soft light across his handsome features, making her heart melt. She’d never stood before him in just a nightgown. He still wore his trousers and shirt and his boots too.

He lowered, kissed her lips and traced his mouth across her cheek, stopping when he reached her ear. “I have pretty words for you, Mrs. Bentley, but you’ll have to pay me a visit if you want to hear them.”

She nodded. “I’d like that very much, Mr. Bentley.”

Chapter Twenty-Six

Hope, The Youngest O'Brian Sister

Hope clutched a crumpled lace handkerchief in one hand, and a novel in the other. She sniffed, trying to hold back the tears that threatened to spill. This was the third time she'd tried to read the chapter and each time she'd dissolved in tears. Her emotions welled up inside her once again. Some things were just too terrible to endure, she concluded, setting the book aside.

"No one should suffer such indignities." Without realizing, she'd said the words aloud. The sound of her voice in the quiet bookshop startled her. Fearing she'd been overheard, she began searching for shoppers. She peered around the dimly lit bookshop, tiptoeing around the shelves to make certain she was alone.

When she found no one, she laughed at her own foolishness and returned to her post. The doorbell rang, and Mrs. Caldicott stepped inside the shop. She liked to pay a visit at least once a week, to hear news of Faith. Too often she brought a gift of candy or fine chocolates she procured at the sweet shop next door.

"Hope, my darling girl, how are you?"

"I was feeling quite distraught, but I'm better now, thanks to you."

Mrs. Caldicott took off her hat but left her gloves on as she always did. She was a very elegant and refined lady, one that Hope admired greatly.

"Why are you distraught?" Mrs. Caldicott set a beribboned box of candy on the counter.

Hope patted the novel she'd just put down. "Jane Eyre. I can hardly stand to read about a poor girl suffering at the hands of others. It's just ghastly."

Mrs. Caldicott frowned at the book. "I believe it has a happy ending, if my memory serves me correctly."

"I don't know if I can endure anymore."

"Well, perhaps you'll feel better to know that I brought your favorite bonbons."

"Bonbons..." Hope laughed. "Just the word makes me hungry. But I need to take care. Mr. and Mrs. Schneider have both told me I'm getting chubby."

Mrs. Caldicott waved a dismissive hand. "Try one."

Hope tugged the ribbon and tossed it aside. "What do I care? I'm never marrying."

"There you go. Everyone knows you're the clever O'Brian," Mrs. Caldicott teased.

Hope studied the chocolates as she considered her words. The box held all sorts of fancy shapes and sizes, but the small chocolate hearts dusted with cocoa were by far her favorite. She didn't dare eat one now, though. If she did, she'd end up with cocoa on her fingers and maybe even her dress. With a pang of regret, she set the top back.

"I better not," she said with a sigh.

"Tell me, have you heard any news from Magnolia?"

"I received a letter just yesterday," Hope said. "A wonderful letter. Faith wrote to say she and Thomas are expecting."

Mrs. Caldicott pressed her hand to her heart. “Oh, my. I can hardly believe it. I know it’s selfish of me, but I’d half-hoped she wouldn’t like Texas and she’d return to civilization to once more be my companion. I miss her so.”

“I do as well,” Hope said, a flurry of emotion coming over her. “The only time I don’t miss my sisters is when I can escape into a book.”

“No thoughts on visiting?”

“I think about it all the time, but if I go, I’ll be outnumbered.”

“What do you mean?”

“Two against one. Grace and Faith will give me no end of grief if I don’t agree to stay and marry that detestable Lucas Bentley.”

Mrs. Caldicott peered over her shoulder into the depths of the shop. “Is someone here?”

“No, I don’t believe so.”

“I just heard someone cough.”

“Nobody’s here. The Schneiders have gone to have lunch with their in-laws. We had several customers earlier, but they’ve all left. I’m alone. Anyway, I’ve decided that I’ll go visit them as soon as the beastly brother-in-law is married.”

“You’re not worried he might pay you a visit and entice you back to Texas, as he promised?”

Hope scoffed. “He didn’t promise to ‘entice me’. He promised far more primitive means, tossing me over his shoulder and whatnot.” She snickered. “He might change his mind if he knew how many bonbons I’ve been eating lately.”

She patted her hip to emphasize her point. Mrs. Caldicott blinked and pinched her lips. Hope felt her cheeks warm with embarrassment. Sometimes she forgot what a fine lady Mrs.

Caldicott was and that she needed to use her best, most ladylike manners.

"You're not fat, darling," Mrs. Caldicott murmured. "You're Rubenesque. And the picture of loveliness. Lucas Bentley would be a very lucky man if you were to accept his proposal of marriage."

"I can't imagine anything less likely. Faith tells me he just bought an enormous parcel of land an hour from Magnolia. He intends to expand his Brahma bull herd."

"Brahma bull?"

Hope shook her head. "Some sort of cattle they say do well in Texas. They're massive creatures."

"How exciting."

"Not to me. They're still cows, and the new ranch doesn't even have a proper house. Not that Lucas and I could ever be compatible. To make matters even worse, he intends to live with the barest necessities. Just a log cabin. A single-room log cabin." She laughed. "Can you imagine?"

To her surprise, Mrs. Caldicott's eyes got a faraway look in them as she seemed to ponder the notion of living in such desperate circumstances.

The subject of Lucas Bentley always made Hope feel a little fretful. She eyed the box of chocolates. With a rush of impulsivity, she snatched one of the dusted chocolate hearts and took a bite.

Mrs. Caldicott smiled. "There you go, dear. When you get to be my age it seems that it's not the things we do that cause us regret. It's the things we don't do." She gestured toward the box. "Have another."

Hope shook her head. "This is wicked, truly. You shouldn't encourage me."

Mrs. Caldicott patted her hand and put her hat on. "I should go. I'm expecting company this afternoon. Dull company, but I need to have tea and refreshments ready, nonetheless. Oh, but I miss your sister!"

Hope saw her to the door and thanked her for stopping by, and for the thoughtful gift. After she shut the door, she turned back, intending to return to the counter. To her shock, a man stood in the shop's main corridor. He was tall, dark-haired and wore a bemused smile. She let out a small yelp, trying to stifle it with her hand, but too late to hold back the desperate sound.

"Sorry," he drawled. "I didn't mean to startle you."

She shook her head, trying to regain her poise. "It's f-fine."

"Wondered if I could get your help with a book?"

"Of course," she whispered.

"It's something my nephew asked me to buy. Maybe you've heard of it?"

Hope sighed with a small degree of relief. The man looked like he'd stepped out of a novel about swashbuckling pirates. Tall, dark, handsome, but slightly roguish too. Not terribly roguish, but somewhat. He wanted to buy a gift for a child, so she had to give him points for that.

"What's the name of the book?" she asked.

He ran his fingers through his hair and frowned. "Something by Jane Austen."

Hope drew a sharp breath. "I love Jane Austen."

"Yes, ma'am. So do I."

"Is it Pride and Prejudice?"

He smiled, his white teeth a stark contrast with his short, dark beard. "You know, I believe that's the very one."

The End

Book Four of Mail Order Bluebonnet Brides
Mail Order Hope

Magnolia, Texas, 1880's - Lucas Bentley needs a wife.

Not because he's lonely. Not because he's in love. If he gets married, in the next two months, he can lay claim to a thousand acres of prime, Texas ranch land.

He decides to pursue the third O'Brian sister in Boston. So far, she has refused to return his letters, ignored him, and some might say, insulted him. But none of that matters now.

He sets off to Boston, planning to court the impossible girl for as long as it takes. Just so it takes less than two days. A perfect plan, if he says so himself.

Books by Charlotte Dearing

<ins>The Bluebonnet Brides Collection</ins>

Mail Order Grace

Mail Order Rescue

Mail Order Faith

Mail Order Hope

Mail Order Destiny

<ins>Brides of Bethany Springs Series</ins>

To Charm a Scarred Cowboy

Kiss of the Texas Maverick

Vow of the Texas Cowboy

The Accidental Mail Order Bride

Starry-Eyed Mail Order Bride

An Inconvenient Mail Order Bride

Amelia's Storm

Mail Order Providence

Mail Order Sarah

Mail Order Ruth

and many others...

Sign up at www.charlottedearing.com to be notified of special offers and announcements.

Printed in Great Britain
by Amazon

39643485R10091